SHERIFF OF SENTINEL

Ben Croft, Sheriff of Sentinel, had too much to do to spend his time riding herd on the spoiled son of the wealthiest rancher around. But when young Jim Taylor's escapades started to involve robbery, gambling debts, and mix-ups with the worst gang of bandits that ever hit the country—why, then Ben Croft made sure he found the time.

For this time all Old Man Taylor's money wouldn't be able to buy the kid out of this tight fix.

Clement Hardin was a pseudonym of **D(wight) B(ennett) Newton** and is the author of a number of notable Western novels. Born in Kansas City, Missouri, Newton went on to complete work for a Master's degree in history at the University of Missouri. From the time he first discovered Max Brand in Street and Smith's *Western Story Magazine,* he knew he wanted to be an author of Western fiction. He began contributing Western stories and novelettes to the Red Circle group of Western pulp magazines published by Newsstand in the late 1930s. During the Second World War, Newton served in the US Army Engineers and fell in love with the central Oregon region when stationed there. He would later become a permanent resident of that state and Oregon frequently serves as the locale for many of his finest novels. As a client of the August Lenniger Literary Agency, Newton found that every time he switched publishers he was given a different byline by his agent. This complicated his visibility. Yet in notable novels from *Range Boss* (1949), the first original novel ever published in a modern paperback edition, through his impressive list of titles for the Double D series from Doubleday, *The Oregon Rifles, Crooked River Canyon,* and *Disaster Creek* among them, he produced a very special kind of Western story. What makes it so special is the combination of characters who seem real and about whom a reader comes to care a great deal and Newton's fundamental humanity, his realization early on (perhaps because of his study of history) that little that happened in the West was ever simple but rather made desperately complicated through the conjunction of numerous opposed forces working at cross purposes. Yet, through all of the turmoil on the frontier, a basic human decency did emerge. It was this which made the American frontier experience so profoundly unique and which produced many of the remarkable human beings to be found in the world of Newton's Western fiction.

SHERIFF OF SENTINEL

Clement Hardin

GUNSMOKE

This hardback edition 2006
by BBC Audiobooks Ltd
by arrangement with
Golden West Literary Agency

ISBN 10: 1 4056 8085 7
ISBN 13: 978 1 405 68085 1

British Library Cataloguing in Publication Data available.

Printed and bound in Great Britain by
Antony Rowe Ltd., Chippenham, Wiltshire

CHAPTER I

THE AIR HELD a nip and smell of autumn, though the sun was warm enough. As Ben Croft unhooked the fastenings of his windbreaker and pushed it back, clearing a holstered gun, sunlight struck brightness from the metal badge pinned to his shirt. The roan gelding under him stomped and jerked at the reins, wanting to drink; Croft gave it rein-length so it could dip its muzzle in the blue-brown water of the creek crossing, where yellow cottonwood leaves drifted down to dapple the sliding surface.

Beside him Homer Ingalls, his deputy, pointed at the mud. "They crossed here, all right—and these prints are fresh. Looks like you outguessed 'em!"

"Not really." The sheriff was scowling ahead to where the trail led steadily upward into a lift of rocks and brush and timber. "It was obvious the ones who took Bud Taylor's horses either had to run them north and west, toward the Deadman, or else come east here past Squaw Head. If they'd taken the Deadman, then there was never any chance at all of our catching up with them. I'd say we were just in luck."

"Have it your way." Ingalls leaned to get rid of a gob-bet of tobacco juice, over his mount's shoulder. Straightening, he wiped a wrist across a brown-stained and drooping gray moustache. "What happens now? We going on?"

Hearing something in his tone, Croft looked at him. "Of course. What else?"

"I dunno. I got a bad feeling. Something's trying to tell me those crooks know we're on their heels."

5

"I wouldn't doubt that a minute. Not if they've kept any watch on their backtrail."

"Then you know they damn well mean to do something about it! And what better place than this?" Ingalls scowled under the gray thicket of his brows at the broken land across the stream. "Anyone that rode into that, it's too good a chance he'd be riding into a trap!"

"I know only one way to find out," Ben Croft said.

"Sure! Go blundering right in and give them a fair shot at you. And by God, I think you'd do it!"

"It happens to be my job."

"You'll get your head blown off, too—all on account of a hunk of tin pinned to your shirtfront. And because somebody run off a few head of riding stock that a gent with Bud Taylor's money won't even miss!"

"If they'd been my horses," Croft pointed out, "I'd have expected the law to do something about it."

"I choose to doubt that! You'd have gone after them yourself—not thrown the thing in somebody else's lap. But why am I arguing?" Ingalls gave a shrug. "I know you well enough to know you'll do what you're going to, and nobody will move you. I just say you're too good a man to throw away. Worth three of a rangehog like Bud Taylor!"

Ben Croft didn't bother to answer. An immense stillness pressed down, broken by the lapping of water and the rustle of dying leaves that dappled this spot with shade and sunlight, as wind moved in the cottonwood branches. With the manner of one who methodically prepares for the next step, the sheriff drew his gun, checked the loads, and then did the same for the rifle in his saddle boot, while Homer Ingalls watched.

"All right," the gray-haired deputy muttered. "What's the program?"

Croft pushed the hat back from his forehead with a thumb. He was a man of about thirty, yellow-haired and sun-darkened, with the level look and the set jaw that marked him as blunt-spoken, direct, and a little stubborn.

6

He had known disappointment and had weathered hard disasters, for which he blamed no one but himself. His tawny moustache would never grow to be as full and long as his older companion's because he had a habit of chewing it when he pondered a problem—as he was doing now, while his pale blue eyes measured the lay of the land in front of him.

"If this is a trap," he said presently, "then it's got to be sprung. Obviously they'll be looking for us to come right in after them, unsuspecting—straight through that gap."

"So?"

"So maybe we can fool them a little." He indicated the broken rock and timber, just above the V-notched pass. "Looks to me a horse could find footing up there. If so, it might be possible to work my way behind them and put them between us."

"You can break your fool neck, too," Ingalls predicted darkly. "What's more, I see a lot of open ground up there, without any cover. Look out or you'll get yourself caught in the open and picked off with a rifle. Like knocking a fly off a windowpane!"

"Yes, there's that," Croft admitted. "But it seems worth a try. Unless you got another suggestion?"

The deputy shrugged. "You damn well know I ain't! So what's my part?"

"I'll want you at this end of the pass, out of sight. Supposing I do manage to flush them into the open, that puts you in position to grab them off."

Homer Ingalls grunted sourly. "You're the boss. . . ."

As Croft sent the roan forward, the ground lifted quickly and at once he was into brush and pine that was choked with slabs of rock fallen from the flank of the mountain above him. He lost the creek and the pass itself, his view narrowing itself now to a matter of yards. But as he climbed the slant grew steeper, and the hampering rocks and growth became more sparse.

The minutes sped. The horse didn't like this and was making heavy work of it, so that Croft had to hold it on a firm rein, stopping from time to time to let it blow. With an outdoorsman's sure instinct for direction, he thought he knew his approximate location. Though he could no longer see the gap, it should be directly below his right stirrup. And now the stunted trees began to thin and suddenly blue sky showed ahead, telling him he was at the lip of the barren slope he'd seen from below. Here Croft reined in, to listen to silence and the faint hum of wind in pine branches.

He stared down toward the far, shadowed end of the pass. If men lurked there, the timber hid them. Ben Croft waited and watched for long minutes, but could see no hint of movement. He lifted his glance then to the open stretch of rubble-strewn slant, which he must somehow negotiate; though it looked steep enough, he saw a deer track that promised footing. Below, the sparest kind of brush screen clung thinly to the rock.

He frowned. As Homer Ingalls had warned, while crossing that he'd be wide open and within easy rifle distance if anyone down there should take his eyes off the gap long enough to look up and see him. Still, there was no other way over and he delayed no longer. He used his spur to move the roan forward, out of the timber fringe.

The horse wanted to balk as soon as it felt rubble start to shift underfoot, but once onto the deer track the going seemed more secure. Feeling like the fly on the window-pane that Ingalls had compared him to, Croft let the animal take its own time; he concentrated on watching the farther trees inch slowly toward him.

Then, halfway over, they struck a soft spot. Loose rock slid and settled, and at once the horse was pawing for traction, sending dirt and rotted rubble streaming and only making things worse. Ben Croft swore and tried to help by throwing his weight forward in the saddle.

But for all its effort the roan was losing; and as it felt its hindquarters begin to slew around, a piercing whicker of sheer terror broke from it.

Something struck and raised a spurt of dust a yard or so

to Croft's left; the crack of a rifle shook its rolling echoes along the cliffs. A bullet from a second rifle down there struck even closer than the first. Well, at any rate Croft had his proof: this had been meant for an ambush!

His hands just then were full with the struggling roan. Fortunately the riflemen hadn't yet got the range and were aiming short; but now the frantic horse lost its footing entirely, and Croft felt his seat start to go from under him. He kicked out of the stirrups, desperately, to keep from being pinned. Sky and rock wheeled. The sheriff landed heavily on elbow and hip, and at once became the center of a small avalanche. He tried to grab at a handful of scrub growth; it was swept from his fingers and he was rolling helplessly, unable to stop himself as a slide of loose rock carried him down.

Then abruptly a clump of rock and brush brought him to a halt and for a moment he could only lie choking on a mouthful of dirt, one palm and a cheek burning as though they had been scraped raw.

With an effort he hauled himself to his knees, aware of a continuing sound of gunfire—and there was the pass, laid out for him and foreshortened as though from a gallery seat in a theater. He could see the ambushers, a pair of them. They were out in the open, rifle barrels bouncing back the sunlight, but they were paying no further attention to him. Instead, at the lower end of the gap, Ben Croft saw what they were shooting at, and he gave a groan.

"The damned fool!" he muttered aloud.

Homer Ingalls was coming in on the spur—straight up into the gap, without any caution at all. Hearing the rifles, and guessing that Croft had run into trouble, Ingalls wouldn't be the man to consider odds or think of anything but bringing help. There was a gun in his fist and as he saw the riflemen he didn't need to be told this was the enemy. He lunged right at them, gun spitting, and one of the ambushers set himself to meet him with weapon braced against hip.

Ben Croft grabbed at his holster—and it was empty. The

9

gun had been scraped out of it in his tumble. Casting about, he saw it snagged in the brush. Hastily he scrambled and snatched it up, shaking the barrel free of dirt, hitting the cylinder a spinning swipe with his palm to make sure the action hadn't clogged. But the fight down there was almost over.

Even as Croft got into position, he saw Homer Ingalls go spilling off the back of his terrified horse. Grimly furious, Croft looked to those who had shot his deputy. It was long range for a handgun, and his fingers trembled with helpless anger; but he steadied his arm on the flat surface of the rock and brought one of those figures into his sights as the man was preparing to give the hurt deputy a finish shot. Croft worked the trigger and, with the kick of the gun against his palm and the sudden burst of muzzle smoke, saw the figure crumple. The rifle went spinning from its grasp.

A bullet whined off the face of the rock that sheltered Croft, as the second ambusher remembered him. He held steady and returned the fire with a pair of bullets which, even at that range and that hastily aimed, must have come too near for comfort. The rifleman back-pedaled and then turned and plunged into the cover of trees, leaving his companion lying where he'd fallen. The guns quit off. Mingled echoes rolled away across the hills and died, and stillness returned.

Frowning, Ben Croft punched out the shells he had emptied and replaced them from the loops of his belt. He saw a stir of movement, narrowed on it and saw that the man he had shot was still alive down there and crawling now—painfully, slowly—for cover. He made a move to raise the gun, then shook his head and lowered it again; he couldn't put a bullet into someone who was already wounded and helpless, horse thief or not.

His own big concern was for Homer Ingalls. Homer might be dead; on the other hand he might be alive but spilling out his blood as the seconds ticked away.

The injured outlaw had pulled himself from sight, leav-

10

ing his rifle on the ground where it had fallen. There was no sign of the second man at all. Yonder, Ingalls' horse had fallen to grazing peacefully; Homer himself wasn't visible to him, from this angle. Suddenly Ben Croft knew he could afford to waste no more time. Turning his head, he looked along the slope for his horse and saw that the roan, having clambered to its feet, had gained the farther trees; he could see it standing motionless, switching its tail, looking as though its reins might have snagged on something to halt its flight. Ben Croft got to his feet, left his boulder and went at a half run across the treacherous slope. He narrowly avoided starting another slide before he reached the trees and firm footing, but he roused no further gunfire. He felt a sudden certainty that he was alone.

The roan had snagged to a blowdown. Croft whipped the reins free, swung into saddle and pointed the animal downslope. As the roan threaded thick jackpine, the sheriff carried his six-gun ready and peered through the shifting trunks for any sign of the enemy, but saw nothing move. Then he hit the level, and at once came upon the tracks left by the band of stolen horses. He turned into the gap where the rear guard had been left to hold up pursuit.

He found blood on the ground but the one he had shot was gone; he guessed that the second man had helped him into his saddle, or simply piled him facedown across it. Just now Croft had no interest in either one of them—or in all the stolen horses in the county. Returning his gun to its holster, he deliberately put his back to the direction the stock thieves had taken, and rode grim-faced to see how it was with Homer Ingalls.

CHAPTER II

THE LAST HOUR was the worst. There were moments when Ben Croft thought he couldn't hold his deputy in the saddle, when it seemed the hurt man would surely lose consciousness and slide out of his hands, and out of the leather, like a half-filled sack of grain. But Homer was game. He swore he would last till they reached town, in spite of pain and the sobering loss of blood from the bullet hole under his ribs. And, somehow, the tough old man actually made it.

They rode into Sentinel just at dusk, something like twenty hours after they'd left it—and with all but a couple of hours of that time having been spent in the saddle. It was Saturday, Croft remembered with the part of his fatigued brain that was still functioning clearly. The town would be starting to come alive with the special fever of a cowtown on the verge of fall roundup. Already men and horses were on the streets, and a racket of celebration and tinny music drifted from the three saloons. Croft avoided all this. He and Homer drifted in through the back streets, their horses brushing stirrups so the sheriff could reach a hand if needed to steady the hurt man. He said, "We made it! Just hang on another minute. I'll take you to my place and send someone for the doctor."

Homer Ingalls, clutching the saddlehorn, lifted his head in protest. "Not that shack of yours! Ain't hardly room for *you* there. I'd crowd you out of house and home."

Croft scowled. "Where else? Doc won't have a place. I got to see you have decent care and looking after."

"I'll be all right. You just take me home."

"To a boardinghouse?"

"Jane Lawry has a crow with a broken wing in a box under her kitchen stove," Homer snapped, in a voice shortened by pain and the fatigue of argument. "Ain't nothing she likes better'n tending critters that's been hurt. She might almost take something off my rent for the privilege. Now will you quit arguing, and move?"

Ben Croft knew the old deputy's real concern was not to make a burden of himself for his employer; still, that shack where Croft kept bachelor quarters had poor facilities for tending anyone as bad hurt as he knew Homer Ingalls to be. The rooming house it would have to be, then. He'd have a word with the landlady, and try to arrange the kind of care Homer needed.

One thing was plain: the old man would have to be got out of that saddle soon, or he would fall out. . . .

The rooming house was a big, two-story affair, neatly painted, with a roofed veranda along two sides and a signboard on the front lawn beside the path. Lamplight showed in windows, upstairs and down. As the horses lagged to a stand a kid went running by, rattling a stick across the fence palings; Ben Croft hailed him.

"Son, I got a hurt man here. Go to the door and fetch Mrs. Lawry or someone." The boy hurried to obey, while Croft tiredly swung down.

Almost immediately, it seemed, the boy was back. The woman he brought with him left the door open and a glow of light silhouetted her faintly, coming hurriedly down the path to the gate. "Why, it's Mr. Ingalls!" she exclaimed.

"Yes, ma'am," said the sheriff.

He scarcely knew the Lawry woman, other than to tip his hat to on the street. She'd been in Sentinel less than a year; she was the widow of an attorney who had come to this Montana countyseat town in search of his health, but who hadn't lived long past hanging out his shingle. Bereft, a thousand miles from any place or anyone she knew, Jane Lawry had nevertheless determined to stay—

13

making a living in the only way she knew, by converting the place her husband left her into a rooming house, and herself into a landlady.

She was still young—twenty-eight perhaps, Ben Croft supposed. In the nature of things it would probably not be long, in a woman-scarce country, before she took another husband. But her loss was still too fresh, probably. She was still disposed to decline all offers.

Croft said, "We ran into some trouble over near Squaw Head. Homer took a bullet; he's lost a lot of blood. I patched him up as best I could and brought him in for the doctor to look at."

"All that distance?" the woman exclaimed. "Quickly! Let's get him down from there and into the house."

"I didn't like to bring him to your place, in this shape," the sheriff said. "But he begged me, and I didn't know where else—"

"And why not? This is his home!" She turned, found the boy, who stood gaping nearby. "Irwin, you go and get the doctor. Don't stop looking till you find him! Hear?"

The youngster hurried off, important with his mission. Ben Croft turned to the task of getting Homer Ingalls down from the saddle of the gray.

Homer was holding onto the saddlehorn with a surprising grip. The sheriff took him by the arm and felt the set of the muscles; when he tried to pull his hand loose the old man resisted, then the arm began to tremble and abruptly Homer Ingalls turned limp and fell forward. The gray snorted its displeasure but was too tired out to do more than sidle a few paces as Croft caught his deputy, and managed to ease him to the ground and get his feet under him.

Then the woman was at Homer's other side, slipping an arm about him. She had surprising strength; she took her share of the hurt man's weight and together she and Croft walked him up the path to the house. Homer Ingalls, mumbling unintelligibly under his breath, tried to help but before they got him across the porch his boots were

14

dragging. Inside the modestly furnished living room he turned automatically toward the stairs but Ben Croft knew they would never be able to get him up there. He looked at Jane Lawry and saw her quick nod of understanding; together they steered Homer toward the horsehair sofa by the fireplace. He collapsed as they reached it.

After that came a period of confused activity. Croft fumbled at the hurt man's clothing while Jane Lawry hurried to the kitchen for clean towels and a basin of boiling water. Homer had quit bleeding, but his shirt and the rag Croft had used as emergency bandaging had stuck to the dried blood around the wound and Ben Croft had to soak the cloth free, working carefully so as not to stain the sofa upholstering or the carpet on the floor.

As he got the angry looking bullet hole laid bare, a hand descended on his shoulder; he looked up to find Sam Elgin standing over him—silver-haired, bespectacled, a look of professional concern on his neat, bearded features. The doctor said brusquely, "All right, Ben, I'll take over now. Why don't you go in the kitchen and let Miz Lawry pour you a cup of coffee? You look about beat out."

Croft refused to budge, in the urgency that crowded him. "That can wait. It's a bad wound, Sam. I don't know how he ever made it home."

"If it was going to kill him," the doctor said patiently, "he'd be a dead man. Now, you do as I tell you, and let me get some work done here."

"All right," Ben Croft said, and pushed to his feet.

He found himself in the kitchen, sitting at an oilcloth-covered table with a mug full of coffee steaming in front of him, and without really knowing quite how either came to be there. He judged from this how exhausted he really was, the reaction hitting him once the responsibility for Homer Ingalls had been lifted from him. The coffee smelled good and he brought it to his mouth and drained off half the cup, in a few quick gulps, before he stopped for breath. It felt good in an empty belly.

He set the cup down, glancing around as Jane Lawry

15

entered from the living room. Reading the question in his eyes she said quickly, "It looks very encouraging. According to Dr. Elgin, it really does."

Croft ran a rope-scarred palm across ragged moustache and whisker stubble, and pushed his fingers through the yellow tangle of his hair. All he could find the words to say was, "That's very good. . . ." He picked up his coffee cup and finished it off, and then stared in surprise as a plate of stew and biscuits was slid in front of him. He looked up quickly. "What's this?"

She said, "You look as though you could use it. I fixed more than I needed. Why don't you sit here and eat, and rest for a few minutes while I help the doctor finish up? The world won't end."

"I got a couple of worn-out horses standing in the street."

"They're taken care of. I told Irwin to take them to the stable. Please . . . I'm sure you haven't eaten since morning. You'll feel better if you get something inside you."

The aroma of the hot food was getting to him. He picked up the fork she had laid beside his plate; holding it he looked at her and mumbled, "Homer always said his landlady was a humdinger. I see what he meant."

Even though they were nearly strangers, her quick answering smile was friendly and without restraint; then she had left him alone again, to his meal. Able at last to relax, he did justice to it, enjoying the comfortable warmth of the kitchen, listening to the tick of a tin clock on a shelf, the occasional rustling of the hurt crow in its box under the stove, the murmur of voices in the living room.

Presently Sam Elgin came bustling in, with the woman carrying the basin of blood-reddened water. As she emptied this, Elgin worked the pump at the sink and washed up; afterward, rolling down his sleeves, he came to the table to tell Ben Croft, "I've done all I can for now. We have to keep him quiet, let him rest. Jane says he can stay right on that couch tonight, which is the best possible thing for him. I'll be back in the morning."

Croft said, "What do you really think?"

16

"I think you both had guts, to try to get clear to town with him. He lost plenty of blood doing it, but you were right to bring him to me as fast as possible. I'd say that if there's no sign of infection by morning he has a good chance."

The sheriff nodded. "Thanks. Send your bill to the county commissioners, Sam. He was shot in line of duty."

"Link Fannin?" the doctor demanded, in a tone that brought him Croft's full attention. The eyes behind the glasses snapped with anger. But Ben Croft had to shake his head.

"I only wish I knew," he said. "I wish I could prove it was Fannin, or some of his crowd—then I could move against them. But I never got a fair look."

"Any real doubt in your mind, though?"

"No," said the sheriff. "But that isn't proof."

The doctor made a sour face as he pulled on his coat. "Someday, somewhere, that border-jumping crook is going to make the wrong play. But the thought doesn't help much now, does it?" He laid an admonishing forefinger on the sheriff's shoulder. "You, my friend, are on the thin edge. . . . Take an old doctor's advice: throw this off your mind and get some rest."

"I won't give you an argument there!" Croft promised. "Now that I know Homer's got the care he needs. Thanks again, Sam."

The doctor nodded and left, taking up his hat and his leather bag from the table where he had set them. The Lawry woman followed him to the front door for last-minute instructions; she returned a moment later, took the plate Ben Croft had emptied, and without asking put in front of him a huge slab of apple pie. He didn't argue, but pitched in on it. She refilled his coffee cup, poured one for herself and took a chair across the table. She sat sipping her coffee and he felt her eyes on him, solemnly observing him. There was no sound from anywhere else in the big, quiet house.

The woman said, "This Link Fannin that you and the

17

doctor spoke of . . . I've heard the name, and I've heard something about him from Homer Ingalls. He's an outlaw?"

"Depends on your definition. He's a horse thief, a rustler, and the boss of a bunch of toughs the like of which we had never seen here around Sentinel, before he moved in. He does everything but boast of the jobs he's pulled all over the state of Montana—yet nobody's ever proved a thing on him. He's that clever." Ben Croft's mouth tightened, and one hand lying on the oilcloth bunched into a fist. "If he thinks he's bringing his operations into my county he's got some more thinking to do!"

Jane Lawry studied his expression. She had a good face, he thought: a generous mouth, serious eyes under a wide brow, smooth brown hair drawn back in wings from a neat center part. She said, "You're very serious about your job."

He shrugged a little, and pushed a morsel of pie crust about the plate with his fork. "Any job deserves to be taken seriously."

"Homer Ingalls always says of you that you do a thing straight right down the line, and no nonsense. He told me something else—in fact, he talks about you a lot. He said you meant to be a rancher, not a lawman. That you were just getting a good start, after four or five lean years, when your herd came down with the fever and you had to destroy them all. And it ruined you."

His brows drew together in a frown. "The risks of the game."

"Yes, the way *you* play it. But Homer told me of a certain neighbor you had, whose herd had been exposed the same as yours. But this man kept his mouth shut, and sold them all to a stranger at a good profit and let him drive them out of the country, to find out in his own time what shape the cattle were in. According to Homer, that was Bud Taylor—the biggest rancher in this valley, the owner of the horses you risked your neck today trying to recover. Something about all this just isn't fair, do you think?"

He looked at her sharply, as though trying to read the

purpose in her questions. He put the last of the pie in his mouth and washed it down with the last of his coffee while he considered his answer.

"I don't claim to be any holier than the next man," he said gruffly. "But I got to live with myself and I want to do it on terms to make me like myself as much as possible. How Bud Taylor runs his affairs is up to Bud Taylor; but his ways ain't necessarily mine.

"Sure, it hurt to lose my spread. Still, there's been satisfaction too, in doing as good a job as I could for the county. Last term, the sheriff retired and the voters promoted me from under-deputy, to fill his shoes. I reckon I'll just go on filling them as best I'm able. And it ain't such a bad life. In fact, I've got so I kind of like it."

He leaned, picked his hat up from the floor where he'd laid it, pushed his chair back. "Mighty good food, ma'am; and mighty nice of you to offer it. Now, like the doc says, I think I better get to bed while there's nothing else hanging over me."

Croft rose, placed the chair against the table. Still seated, the woman said, "I'm sure Homer Ingalls is going to be all right. But if it would make you feel better to be near him, his room will be empty tonight. Would you like to sleep there?"

He hesitated, then nodded. "I'd like to very much. If you promise you'll wake me if he needs me for anything."

"I promise," she said. "The room is the one to the right, at the head of the steps. Make yourself at home. And rest well...."

"Thanks," he said again, and left her.

CHAPTER III

HE CAME AWAKE in confusion, pawing up through cottony layers of sleep to find himself in a strange bed, with sunlight slanting in at him from an unfamiliar angle. Then it came to him that the bed, and the window, were in Homer Ingalls' room, and he remembered what he was doing here. At the same moment he heard again the urgent tapping at the door that had roused him. He sat up abruptly as Jane Lawry's voice spoke his name. She asked, "Are you awake?"

"Yeah," he said gruffly. "What's wrong? Is it Homer? Is he worse?"

"No, no," she answered quickly through the closed door. "He's sleeping quietly. But someone's come for you. I'm afraid there's been some trouble."

"I'll be right out." He was already reaching for his trousers, on a chair by the bed.

His big silver watch showed the hour as nine o'clock—the latest he had slept in years, even on a quiet Sunday morning such as this one. It was a measure of the amount of physical and nervous energy yesterday's doings had drained from him. He dressed hurriedly, pausing to peer at his reflection in the mirror as he passed a hand across two-day-old beard bristles. A shave would have to wait. He didn't know what was afoot this morning, but obviously it was something urgent.

Downstairs he had a look at the sleeping Homer Ingalls and satisfied himself that his deputy had got through the night as well as he could have hoped. Jane Lawry, looking competent and fresh in a house dress and apron and none the worse for any sleep she might have lost because of her patient, nodded toward the front door. "I had the man wait outside," she said in a half whisper. "So as not to disturb him."

"Thanks," Croft said, and walked out pulling on his coat and hat.

There had been some rain during the night, and a pleasant smell of damp earth hung heavy in the air. On the porch, a puncher from one of the valley ranches, a fellow named Rayburn, prowled about impatiently. "How'd you know where to find me?" Croft asked.

"Something Doc Elgin said."

The sheriff picked that up quickly. "The doc? Is somebody hurt?"

"Fred Houk," the puncher said. "He's been slugged and robbed."

"The devil you say! Where'd this happen?"

"Back room of his store."

Croft swore but asked no more questions. He was already heading for the heart of town, with his long, ground-covering stride. The other man fell in beside him.

Houk's was a general mercantile, dealing in everything from yard goods and jeans to saddles and barb wire—a capacious building constructed of logs, with a tin roof that reflected an eye-aching smear of morning sunlight; it dominated one block of Sentinel's main street. On Sunday, of course, it was closed for business, but rumors of violence had drawn a curious cluster of people. When they saw the sheriff they descended on him with excited questions, which Croft merely shrugged aside. The door was opened to him by the storekeeper's wife. With Rayburn still dogging him, he went on through the main body of the store and past a curtained doorway to a room at the back that served Fred Houk for an office.

It was hardly more than a cubbyhole, furnished with a battered desk and chair and a wooden file cabinet that had a harness company's calendar on the wall above it. A door

21

opened on a supply room, another onto the alley at the back. There was one dusty-paned window, and a small iron-bellied stove that had been lit against the chill of the autumn morning, and was pouring out heat until the room was nearly stifling.

Fred Houk, a pale-skinned man turning flabby with middle age and lack of proper exercise, sat in the chair at the desk; his head was swathed in bandages and his eyes had the dull, unfocused glaze of shock. Sam Elgin, with coat off and sleeves rolled to the elbow, was packing his instruments away in his leather bag. The desk, and the floor around it, held a litter of account books and invoices and other papers that looked as though they had been scattered in some sort of a scuffle.

Five people filled the room. As Mrs. Houk, a harried-looking woman who looked older than her husband, ushered him and Rayburn inside, Ben Croft walked over and closed the draft of the stove that no one had thought of checking. He looked at the man slumped against the desk and asked the doctor, "Is Fred bad hurt?"

"Someone used a gun barrel on him," Elgin said brusquely. "Could have caved his skull; as it is I think he has a concussion. He's going to be kind of a sick man for a few days."

"Can he tell us what happened?"

Elgin shrugged while the woman wrung her shaking hands. Then the storekeeper stirred and lifted his head; his wavering glance sought Ben Croft and he said, in a voice that sounded dull with effort, "Sheriff? He tried to kill me—and he took the cash box. Near three hundred dollars in it."

"Who was he?"

The man only shook his head. "I came down this morning to catch up on my bookwork. I was sitting right here at the desk. Never heard the alley door open—had no idea he was in the room until he was on top of me. When I tried to get to my feet he hit me. Felt like my head exploded...."

22

Art Rayburn spoke up. "Whoever it was, looks like the damn fool had his gun cocked; it jarred off when he pole-axed Houk, and the shot brought a bunch of us running. So, he just grabbed the cash box and beat it out the alley."

"Just how long ago was this?" Croft demanded.

Rayburn looked at the doctor as the latter said, "Couldn't have been more than fifteen, twenty minutes. A gunshot, on a Sunday morning, is enough to rouse this town pretty quick. Somebody fetched me, and I told them to look for you at Jane Lawry's."

Croft nodded shortly. He rubbed his hand across the wiry stubble of unshaven beard, trying to shake the bone-deep tiredness that still remained in him after his night's rest. He thought, *I feel like an old man; I feel nearly as old as Homer Ingalls. And I'm thirty-five years younger!*

He shook himself out of this mood, saying gruffly, "Guess I better go to work. Art, while I'm having a look in the alley, would you go down to the livery stable for me? Tell Charlie I want the sorrel. He knows which is my rig."

As the puncher hurried away, Houk roused himself enough from his stupor to clutch at Croft's sleeve; concern for his loss honed a gleam in the dull glaze of his eyes. "Get him, Sheriff! He took three hundred dollars from me. Get it back, if you have to kill the bastard! You hear me?"

"I hear!" Croft grunted, and pulled his arm free. Three hundred dollars appeared to look bigger to Houk than a man's life, perhaps even, than his own.

In the cindered alley behind the store, Croft found the first clue by blind luck. There had already been a number of curious people milling around back here, kids mostly, trying to peer through the window of Houk's office and see something of what went on inside; among them they had managed to trample out any sign there might have been near the store entrance. But some yards away, as he rode slowly up the alley on the sorrel that had been brought for him, he discovered the overturned rainbarrel.

23

It normally stood at the rear corner of the feed store, adjacent to Houk's, and it had been fairly full of runoff from the gutterspout when something knocked it over. Ben Croft, on a hunch, looked and found the iron shoe prints in the mud formed by its spilling.

He could almost picture the scene: in his hurry to escape, Houk's assailant must have transmitted some of his own panic to his waiting horse. Precious moments would have been lost in mounting: the man sweating and cursing and trying to hold onto the stolen money box, the animal acting up and fighting the reins. And so the barrel had been tipped; and going down for a closer look, Croft quickly sorted out the overlapping hoofprints and discovered one—the print of a right shoe with a twisted frog, clearly repeated a number of times—that to a horseman was as distinctive a mark as any signature or thumbprint.

Until that shoe was replaced, he knew, he would be able to identify the horse that wore it beyond any reasonable sort of doubt.

The fugitive, having straightened out his mount, had spurred it along the alley on the quickest route possible out of town. The prints were quickly lost in scattered cinders. But Ben Croft was in no great hurry as he swung again into the saddle, and set himself to follow.

After the night's rain, the sky was a field of broken clouds and the land lay mottled with their shadows, steaming faintly where the sun touched it. Ben Croft quickly struck the main valley road that cut almost due north, serving the ranches that lay in this section of the range. It being Sunday morning, and still fairly early, there would have been little travel over that road as yet. Thanks to this and to the rain, its surface should hold good sign.

Sure enough, it took no time at all to discover the mark of the shoe with the twisted frog. It was all so easy that Croft began to wonder if it might be *too* easy. Whoever had committed assault and robbery on Fred Houk seemed to have done an astonishingly stupid job of it.

Presently the road skirted a clump of jackpine; he approached with caution, remembering what had happened at Squaw Head Pass and determined not to be led into ambush twice in two days. There was plainly no one lurking among the shifting trunks of the trees, however; but in making sure of it he forgot to watch the road and had ridden on some distance before he realized he had lost the tracks. Croft swore tiredly as he hauled around and rode back, searching.

He saw he'd been partly right after all. The fugitive had turned aside here, into the trees; though there were no tracks, Croft found where a horse had been kept standing— for some little time, to judge from the scuffed-up needle litter. Here also he found the butt of a smoked-down cigarette. Probably for the time it took him to roll and consume that cigarette, the fugitive had held up here to learn if anyone might be following. From this point the tracks led north and east across the open, toward a region of low and rolling grassy hills.

Putting his sorrel in that direction, Croft debated whether the man had ridden on because of a certainty his backtrail was clear, or rather because he'd caught sight of the sheriff coming. He decided, tentatively, that it wasn't the latter. The rider seemed to be taking his time, like one with no particular pressures on him.

Croft began to feel that he must be perhaps half an hour behind his man. That was no great lead. The thought made him pull his gun as he rode, roll the cylinder for a check of the loads and then drop it back into holster again. Satisfied in his methodical way that it was ready when he might need it, he touched up the horse with a spur barb, determined to get on with this thing and have it over.

Still he didn't crowd his man, because that was the surest way to risk overrunning the trail and losing it, as he'd almost done once already. Yet even so he nearly missed the dull glint of metal lodged in the heart of a wild rose bush, growing on a creekbank; pulling rein he swung down and, collecting a couple of scratches as he did so, dragged out the black tin cash box. The lock had been forced and

25

the box was empty. The thief had rifled it, no doubt while waiting for his horse to drink, and tossed it away. Damned careless, Ben Croft thought, about getting rid of evidence. The sheriff took long enough to fasten the thing to a saddle string, and then swung astride again and sent his sorrel down into the creek.

As he crossed it and picked up the trail again on the opposite bank, he was beginning to wonder still more about the intelligence of the person he was chasing.

The tracks led into some outcroppings, but probably less from an attempt to lose them in the broken rocks than simply because these happened to lie on the route. Croft was held up scarcely at all. He was in a section of range that he knew perfectly well—so well, in fact, that as he saw how steadily the tracks continued to bear on a direct line, east by a little north, he found himself starting to grow vaguely alarmed.

When, presently, he topped over into a long, gentle swale and saw the buildings of a ranch before him, Croft reined in.

It was a modest layout, hardly more than a one-man operation, backed by a windbreak of tall cottonwoods. The house had been there for some time, with lean-to enlargements tacked on as need demanded; but the barn—beyond the house and partly hidden by it—was large and well constructed and almost new, taking the place of one that had burnt some half dozen years before. The shingles and siding looked hardly even weathered. Ben Croft knew precisely how old the barn was: he had built it himself, with his own hands. This ranch had been his once, before the blackleg got into his beef herd and put at least temporary end to his ambitions of being a cattleman.

And this was where the tracks led. He would learn nothing by sitting here puzzling about them. He knew only one way of finding out what it meant: the direct way, of riding down there. He shook out his bridle, and sent the sorrel on.

CHAPTER IV

COFFEE CUP in one hand and meat sandwich in the other, the dark-headed young man had drifted over to the window; suddenly he tensed. The girl slicing bread at the kitchen table looked up with a start as she heard him swear. "Why, Jim! What is it?"

His eyes were hard, his smooth cheek muscles bunched. "*You* take a look!" he said roughly around a mouthful of bread and beef. "Looks to me like our brave sheriff!"

She put down her knife and joined him. Her bright blond head came barely to his chin as she peered out across the sweep of grass at the approaching rider. "Why, it *is* Ben Croft!" she exclaimed. "I wonder what he'd want here?"

"Yeah, I wonder!" The girl, still at the window, missed the panic that moved fleetingly across the young fellow's brooding stare. He drained his china cup and set it down, the spoon rattling; a hand dropped, briefly, to touch the place where a holstered gun would have been strapped against his leg, except that his shellbelt was hanging now from the pommel of the horse standing ground-hitched outside the door.

He said harshly, "If *you* don't know what he's doing here, then just who would?"

China blue eyes turned on him in astonishment. "Why, Jim Taylor! You're not *jealous?* Are you thinking I've been seeing Ben behind your back?"

"What else am I supposed to think? He knows your pa ain't home, so *that* ain't who he came to see!"

Edie Bishop couldn't look like anything but a pretty blond girl, however angry she might be. Now her red lips pouted and she pushed the fair hair back from her forehead. "And what would there be wrong in me liking Ben Croft?" she demanded. "I've known him just as long as I have you. He's a brave man, and a real handsome one."

"He's nothing!" Jim Taylor retorted. "He never was able to make a go of this spread that your folks finally took over. I'll wager you the nickel in the badge on his chest is worth more than everything else he owns—and *it* belongs to the county!"

She tossed her head. "I don't see what difference that should make."

"Then go right ahead, if he's what you want!" the man said with a shrug. "There's plenty other girls around, who'd know better than to pick a ragged-pants sheriff over the man that'll one day be owning the biggest ranch in the county!"

The threat was enough to warn her she had pushed him too far; she dropped her coquettishness and one small paw clutched anxiously at his coat sleeve. "Now, Jim, you know I'm only teasing! *I* don't know why Ben Croft would be coming here. I certainly never asked him!"

"Then get rid of him!" Another glance at the rider, drawing much closer now, set Jim Taylor wheeling toward the door. He plucked an expensive, flat-topped black hat off the knob of a chair as he passed. "Your pa being away," he said, "it's just as well if he don't find out I'm here. No telling what kind of talk could spread."

"You can't imagine Ben Croft would be the sort to start dirty stories going about us!"

"If he was jealous enough, I wouldn't put it past him!" Jim Taylor pulled on the hat, laid his hand on the doorknob. "I'm moving my horse into the barn where he can't see it. You make him believe you're alone, you hear? And don't let him light, not if you care anything about seeing much of *me* around here in the future!"

28

Her hands clasped anxiously. "Don't be that way, Jim! Please!"

But he was already gone, the door slamming behind him. She stared helplessly after him. She might have been puzzled if she could have seen the expression of panic on his face.

Ben Croft, riding in toward the quiet buildings of what had once been his own place, watched for some sign of activity. There was a blue pencil line of smoke rising idly from the mud-and-stone chimney of the house. The leaves of the cottonwoods, freshened by last night's rain, twinkled brightly; windmill blades made a smear of sunlight. But when he came around the corner of the house and the yard opened up in front of him, he could see nothing move except for a pair of unsaddled horses in the pole corral.

Neither horse showed the dark markings of sweat, or any other sign that they had been ridden recently. The work area of the yard itself was hardpan, tramped solid by many hooves, and such rain as they'd had last night would only turn it greasy, without softening it enough to show tracks. It began to look as though he had drawn a blank.

Yet, damn it, nothing could change the fact he had followed a rider straight to this ranch. He didn't believe the man could have had time to ride further. No, he had to be here.

As Croft pulled up and rubbed a fist across his tawny moustache, puzzling over things, the kitchen door suddenly opened. Edie Bishop came out upon the stoop, and closed the door behind her. She pushed at her wealth of golden curls as she exclaimed brightly, "Why, hello, Ben. What in the world are you doing out this way?"

As always when he was near her Croft felt the pulse slogging a little faster in his throat. From the day two years ago when she came to this country with her father, to take over the spread Ben Croft had lost through his disastrous experience with blackleg, Edie Bishop had filled his thoughts to the exclusion of any other woman. That her young blond loveliness seemed distantly unobtainable—certainly, for a man trying to fight his way back from economic defeat—only made her that much more attractive.

"Did you want to see Papa?" Her voice, he thought, held an oddly tremulous note; her hands made birdlike gestures to smooth the apron across her trim and rounded hips. "I'm afraid he's not home. He rode over to see a man at Flynn's Creek on Thursday."

"I knew that," Croft told her. "I figured you'd be alone. That's why I was some concerned."

"About me?" Blue eyes widened. "But what on earth for, Ben? What could possibly happen?"

He sensed a false note. She continued to smile at him, and yet the smile and the easy friendliness of her voice were not quite true. Suddenly an alarming thought brought his attention to the windows of the house. They returned his stare blankly. Dissatisfied, he eased the sorrel a couple of steps nearer the porch and leaned as though to examine a bridle piece, as he spoke to the girl in a voice he hoped would carry no further than her own ears: "If there's someone in the house—with a gun, maybe, keeping us both covered—just nod your head. . . ."

Her eyes only widened in genuine astonishment. "I can't imagine what you're talking about! Of course there's nobody! Would you like to come in and look for yourself?"

Ben Croft only shook his head, convinced and relieved to know he had guessed wrong. Plainly she was in no peril, then; whatever the cause of her strange behavior, it wasn't that. "Sorry," he said gruffly. "It was only a notion, and I had to be sure." He pulled off his hat briefly and ran the fingers of one hand through his stiff, tawny mop of hair. With his jaws shagged by unshaven beard, he knew he made a poor sight and he bitterly regretted that she must see him this way. Dragging the hat on again, he explained briefly: "We had some trouble in town this morning. Fred Houk was waylaid in his office at the store, and robbed of three hundred dollars. I'm on the trail of the man who did it."

Edie Bishop's mouth formed a round O. She exclaimed, "And you thought for some reason he might be *here?*"

"He has to be here somewhere. This is where the sign leads. I even found the box the money was in. . . . But you're sure you haven't seen any strangers? Or any one at all?"

"No one at all," she insisted, a shade too quickly.

There was no use, he decided, trying to understand just what made her act so strangely; he would not press her. He still faced the inescapable fact that the fugitive had ridden this way, and that he could have hardly ridden further. Ben Croft straightened in the saddle, and ran a slow look around the perimeter of the yard with its scatter of outbuildings, all standing silent under the October sun.

"It's altogether possible," he said, "the man could have sneaked in and you not know. Call it a hunch, but he could be lying low right now, just hoping I'll go on without spotting him. If it's all the same to you, Edie, I think it wouldn't hurt if I had a look around. The barn, anyway."

This time there was no mistaking the sudden indrawn breath that lifted her rounded bosom, or the smothered alarm in her voice as she protested. "But, Ben! I've told you . . . you'll only be wasting your time! There's nothing at all in the barn. Can't you take my word for it?"

"Sorry," he said again. "I've been wrong before, and I expect to be again. But this time I've got a feeling." And leaving her standing there, he pulled the rein that started his sorrel at a walk across the hard-packed dirt of the yard, toward the big barn. He heard a single muffled word from the girl but he deliberately paid no mind to it.

Before the barn he stepped out of saddle, ground-hitched the sorrel and drew his gun as he turned to look at the big door. He knew every detail of the building's interior, his having been the brain that designed it and the hands that did the work of construction. Now, as he reached for the latch, from within came the sudden, unmistakable sound of a shod hoof striking timber. Not hesitating, Ben Croft jerked the ponderous door wide enough to hurl himself around the edge of it, lunging for the shadows of the interior.

He half expected to meet a bullet, but none came; hugging the rough wall, with the breath clamped inside his lungs, he felt an itching dampness of sweat spring out beneath his shirt. The partially open door let in some light, but the rear half of the building was lost in gloom, and the stillness smelled of hay and horses, mice and leather. As his eyes became adjusted Croft searched the corners for any hint of movement.

Then, in one of a row of stalls along the left wall of the barn, the strike of iron shoe against a partition sounded for a second time. Grip tightening on his gun, the sheriff started that way at a half-crouch.

He reached the stall without mishap and slipped into it, alongside the buckskin that was tied there. For all he could tell to the contrary, they could be the only living creatures in the barn's smothering stillness. The animal was under saddle but it was too dark to see much more than that. Croft's hand, exploring, discovered a shellbelt looped over the saddlehorn; there was also a holster—empty. He registered this fact as his palm moved on to the animal's flank, and found warmth that told him it had been very recently ridden.

He felt scar tissue of a branding iron then, and tracing it with his fingers made out the shape of a Diamond T—Bud Taylor's brand! Croft wasn't too surprised, however. A good percentage of the horses in the county belonged to its biggest rancher. He could assume that this one was stolen. Going down on his ankles, he induced the animal to raise its left rear leg and, again by touch, read the shoe. He didn't have to see the iron to know he had found what he was looking for: beyond any question this was the same twisted frog that had laid its mark in the mud of the alley behind the Houk store, and had led Croft directly to a shadowed stall in Warren Bishop's barn.

Slowly he straightened, every nerve stretched and alert. He moved out of the stall again, into the narrow aisle—and at that moment heard and felt the rush of a body hurtling toward him.

Even as he whirled to meet the attack, he realized that the man had been hidden behind a partition that separated off an area used for storing gear and tools. He saw an arm descending, the metal of a gun barrel gleaming dimly; he remembered the clubbing blow that had laid out Fred Houk and ducked away from it, and his boot slipped in loose straw and sent him stumbling to one knee.

His attacker, lunging forward, collided with him and he felt the blow of the forearm strike glancingly across his shoulders, the gun barrel widely missing its mark. The man grunted, his breath warm on Croft's ear. Then the sheriff got traction under one bootsole and he drove upward, hurling the other off him and bulling him back to slam against the timbers of the partition while the gun was dislodged and sent spinning from his fingers.

It must have been on cock, for striking the floorboards jarred off an explosion, a shock of sound in the echoing barn that made the buckskin squeal in terror. Ben Croft's assailant started to sidle away, with a scrape of clothing against rough wood. The sheriff, his ears ringing, lunged after him and saw the steel teeth of a pitchfork that the man had somehow managed to grab up. The points were aimed squarely at his chest but he never faltered. His left hand reached and shunted the ugly tines aside, and then he was on the other and had him backed into the partition, the barrel of his own six-shooter laid against his throat. Hoarse with anger, he gritted, "All right, damn you! Freeze!"

"*Don't shoot!*" Terror had the breath whistling in the man's throat. The fork dropped from his hands with a clatter; to steady him Croft caught a handful of his coat-

33

front and shoved him up against the wood, hard. The hat tumbled to the floor.

He got his first real look at the face of his prisoner, then, and a grunt of disbelief broke from his lungs. So great was his astonishment that he let go and stepped back a pace, staring in the dim light. Drifting smoke from that single explosion of gunpowder stung his nose.

Jim Taylor glared back at him. There was sweat on the young fellow's spoiled and handsome face; his lips were pulled away from his teeth and he still hadn't got full control of his breathing. "Damn you, Croft!" he gritted. "What's the idea, laying hands on me?"

For a moment the sheriff was unable to answer; that the one he had chased here to Bishop's could be Bud Taylor's son was so incredible, he could only believe he must have made some monstrous error. But then his jaw hardened beneath the tawny moustache. "I could ask you why you tried to brain me with that gun barrel!"

The other man had an answer. "How was I to know who you were? To me, it looked like you were trying to sneak my horse!"

All the uncertainty left Croft, then. Incredible or not, he had made no mistake. "So that *is* your horse? You rode him here?"

"He's got my pa's brand, ain't he? And he's carrying my saddle."

Coldly Croft looked his prisoner over. He was slim, well built, some five years younger than the sheriff; his dark good looks came from his mother, not from the hard-bitten cattle boss who had sired him. Croft had known him for most of both their lives, and he was secretly of the opinion that too much money had been spent on Jim Taylor, and not well spent either. His canvas coat and whipcord breeches were specially cut for him, his boots bench-made and soft as glove leather; the shirt that showed through the opening of his coat had pearl buttons and piping at the edges of the pockets.

Something bulged one of those pockets. Without warning

34

Ben Croft shoved in a hand and brought forth what he had known he would find—it was a good, thick roll of greenbacks.

Jim Taylor let out a yell. "What do you think you're doing?"

"Collecting evidence," Croft answered shortly. "This is what you took off Fred Houk when you broke into the store this morning."

Taylor gave a bellow of fury. "The hell it is! Give it here!" He made a grab for the roll of money but Croft simply shoved him back against the partition.

"You've played the fool enough for one day," the sheriff said. "Now simmer down. We're taking this money back where it belongs." Stowing it away in his own clothing, he turned and saw the gun Taylor had lost in the scuffle. He picked it up and stuffed it behind his own waistband; then he led the buckskin out of its stall. Jim Taylor stood with lowered head, eyes blazing and furious, seemingly beyond speech. His expensive, flat-topped hat with the silver ornaments around the band lay at his feet; coolly Ben Croft got it and thrust it into his hand and said, "Let's go."

The younger man found his tongue. Voice trembling, he said, "You're way out of line, Croft. You do this, and my pa will have that badge. I'm not fooling!"

Croft looked at him. "Neither am I," he retorted. "Nor is the judge going to be, when he hears the case against you! Damned if I can fathom why you'd take it into your head to hold up a store; but for the moment, I just ain't interested in your reason. I don't even care that your pa is Bud Taylor. . . . I nearly lost my deputy yesterday, trying to bring back some of Bud Taylor's horses for him, not that we expected any thanks. Right now, I'm just a little bit sick of the Taylor family!

"So you walk out of here in front of me. I'd suggest you don't give me any trouble!"

CHAPTER V

EDIE BISHOP was waiting for them outside the barn; after that gunshot, her face was chalk white and her hands knotted tightly together. "Jim, are you all right?" she cried. "I swear I never told—" Then the looks on their faces, and the gun in Ben Croft's hand, seemed to register. She sucked in a quick breath. "What—what's happening?"

Taylor, his sweaty face flushed and angry, only brushed her with a glance. Ben Croft felt a sick disappointment as he looked at the girl, realizing she had deliberately lied to him—had known all the time that Taylor was in the barn. For a terrible moment he wondered if she had known about the robbery, too, then from her wide-eyed and genuine confusion decided no, she couldn't have. Still, he didn't trust himself to speak; he brushed aside her stammered question and, dropping the buckskin's reins, turned to his own waiting horse and lifted into the saddle.

"Mount up!" he told his prisoner gruffly.

Taylor looked as though he wanted to argue, but after a look at Croft's face he clamped his jaw tight and sullenly obeyed. Edie Bishop found her voice again; she cried, "Will one of you please tell me what this is all about?" She took a step toward the prisoner, a hand lifted in frightened appeal.

Croft's mouth pulled down sourly under the ragged moustache and he said, "Get away from him, Edie. He's under arrest. I'm taking him in."

"What it means," Jim Taylor told her, "is that our sheriff is making the biggest damn fool mistake of his life. Believe me, he'll find that out!"

36

She shook her head, stammering helplessly. Not trusting himself to say any more to her, Croft gave his prisoner an order and they went out of the ranch yard. They left the girl standing there, bewildered and unhappy, with the ground breeze tugging at her skirt and whipping a golden strand of hair it had worked loose.

Jim Taylor saw Croft's bleak expression and told him, "Don't think you'll be making a hero of yourself in her eyes, with what you're doing! In case you never noticed, I got the inside track there."

The sheriff ground his jaws but made no answer. He knew too well that was true. He'd long sensed Edie's partiality for this good-looking fellow; it was something he'd had to accept. After all, Jim Taylor had a lot about him to attract a woman, aside from the obvious advantage of his father's wealth. And Ben Croft, who was strictly a workhorse with little time to spare from his job and few gifts of charm or flattery, knew his own failings. He had had to stand on the sidelines at too many dances, in the hall above the courtoom in town, and swallow his jealousy as he watched the girl he loved swing lightly by in Taylor's arms, aware that he knew too little of dancing to risk trying to cut in.

It really hurt, though, to have her deliberately lie to him. He knew perfectly well now that Taylor had seen him coming and had hidden in the barn, after warning Edie not to betray him; and the girl, not hesitating to question his motives, had done exactly what she was told. . . .

The miles fell away. With Sentinel less than a half hour distant, Jim Taylor suddenly broke a silence neither man had disturbed since leaving Bishop's. His voice held an edge of strain as he whipped his head around and, above the noise of the horses, said suddenly, "All right, damn you! I know what the county pays you for that stinking sheriff's job. There's better than two months' salary in that roll in your pocket. All you have to do to keep it, say you turned up a blank and missed the trail."

Hearing this, Ben Croft hauled rein so abruptly that the sorrel under him shook its head in protest. He felt the stiffness of his mouth and heard the anger shake his voice as he glared at the other man and told him, "I always knew you were a sonofabitch, Jim—but at least I thought you were above trying to give me a bribe! One more word like that, and I'll haul you out of the saddle and pound the whey out of you!"

"Maybe you want to try?" Taylor challenged; but then he turned sullen, his eyes hooding behind their lids as he settled deeper into the leather. "Go to hell!"

They rode the rest of the way in an unbroken, dangerous silence.

Ben Croft was hoping not to have an audience when he brought Bud Taylor's boy into jail, and he very nearly made it. The Sunday streets were quiet; the excitement over this morning's robbery had apparently had time to simmer down. Now, at midday, there was no traffic along the main street. But when Croft and his prisoner turned off into the sidestreet that contained the sheriff's office and jail, a Diamond T puncher shouldered out through the swing doors of the hotel bar. He halted on the roofed veranda to watch them go by, and Croft was sure that a look, and a signal, passed between the man and his prisoner.

Now as Croft racked his sorrel before the jail and ordered Jim to dismount, the man standing in shadow on the hotel porch started toward them down the steps. He came straight over the dust of the wide crossing, walking fast. Ben Croft, ignoring him, took a key from his pocket and unlocked the office door. He heard his name spoken, a challenging shout, but he didn't look around, merely put a hand on Jim Taylor's shoulder and prodded him inside.

The sheriff's office, like the man himself, was unprepossessing, tidy, and businesslike. Everything had its place. Reward posters were neatly filed, the current ones on a spindle on the desk. The corners were swept, the spittoon emptied but kept handy as a reminder to visitors they were not to use the floor. The stove had had a recent blacking, the windowglass was free of flyspecks; the jail arsenal—a carbine, a pump-action shotgun, and a brace of six-shooters that had been taken from prisoners and never reclaimed— were under lock and key. In one corner, the cot where Croft or his deputy slept when they had a prisoner in the cell was neatly made.

The jail's single cell occupied a corner of the room, framed in good metal bars with a solid steel door. Croft got the keyring off a wall peg, ushered Taylor inside and slammed the door on him. He was just turning the key in the heavy lock when boots struck the plank walk out- side, and the man from the bar lunged into the room. Croft deliberately removed the key before turning to face him.

"Something you wanted, Keel?" he asked flatly.

Mort Keel stood with head thrust forward on chunky shoulders, peering from the sheriff to the prisoner in the cell. The Diamond T puncher had a head like a bullet, sandy hair so short-cropped and fine as to be scarcely visible, and a face scarred by countless bunkhouse brawls. He looked at his employer's son clutching the bars of the cell and he demanded harshly, "What is this, Croft? Some kind of a joke?"

"The charge," Croft told him, "is assault and robbery. The judge will have to decide whether it's a joke or not."

"Damned fool thinks he can actually hold me in here!" Jim Taylor spoke up. "He says I took three hundred dollars off of Fred Houk this morning. I've been telling him he's made the mistake of his life."

The puncher rubbed a fist across his mouth and then dropped the arm to his side. He had a rubber-butted six- shooter in a cutaway holster strapped against his leg. Ben Croft let his hand rest on the butt of his own gun, not drawing it, and he said, "I suggest you go about your busi- ness."

Mort Keel's eyes narrowed on the sheriff's gunhand. He looked again at the man in the cell. "I'll get on out to the ranch. Don't worry, kid. When Bud hears about this, he'll tear the damn jail down brick by brick, if he has to, but he'll have you out of there." His eyes swiveled back to the sheriff. "That should give you about an hour to change your mind and turn him loose . . . if you got any brains at all!"

He heeled about and took his slabby shape out of the doorway; sound of his boots on the loose boardwalk quickly faded, as he hurried back to where his horse had been left in front of the hotel. Behind Croft, Jim Taylor said tensely, "All right, damn you! You'll see what happens when my pa gets here. And remember, you asked for it!"

Croft gave him a look, but no answer.

As Keel had said, he probably had an hour. He put young Taylor's gun away in a drawer of the desk, together with the three hundred dollars, and locked it. Afterward he built a fire in the heater to take off the chill of the fall day. He set water on to warm and got out the razor he kept in his desk, and scraped away at a wiry thicket of whiskers. Afterward, with cheeks stinging from the razor's pull, he picked up the tin cash box and went out, locking the door and leaving Jim Taylor stretched out on the bunk in the cell, sullenly waiting for his father.

Apparently the town was unaware of the arrest; nobody greeted Croft with questions as he got into his saddle and, leading young Taylor's horse, rode back into Main Street and there turned a half block to the public livery and corral. The old barn hostler got up from his barrel chair before the stable door and came to greet him, limping badly on a leg that was twisted and badly healed from a riding accident that had ended his years as a saddleman. He took the reins of both horses as Croft swung down. "I seen you and the Taylor boy riding in," he said. He looked at the buckskin with the Diamond T brand, and his glance kindled with curiosity. "What about this one? This a county charge?"

"No," Ben Croft said shortly. "Put it on Bud Taylor's bill." He offered no explanation and the old man seemed to

40

know from his expression that there was no use expecting one. The sheriff started to walk away, then thought of something and turned back. "Charlie, you can do me a favor. I guess there's nobody has an eye as sharp as yours for spotting riders that come into this town."

"I keep track of things," Charlie agreed modestly. "Sitting here, what else I got to do with my time?" He added, "What's the favor?"

"You know Link Fannin when you see him?"

The corners of the old man's mouth pulled down hard. "That damned cattle rustler? I reckon! Nobody else ever had his kind of gall—to move that longrider crew in on a decent range like this one, and just make himself to home!" The old hostler spat into the dust. "And the whole time, laughing in our faces! The man knows damn well all Montana savvies what he is, even if he's never made the mistake of letting anyone prove it on him!

"Can't say, though, that I've seen him or his crew around right lately," Charlie went on thoughtfully. "Not in the last few days."

"I didn't suppose you had," Croft said. "I got reasons to think he's been busy. But anyhow, next time you do see him, I'd appreciate it if you'd get word to me. Right away."

The faded eyes narrowed. "You aim to tangle with Link Fannin?"

"I aim to tell him a few things. You'll let me know if he shows?"

He got Charlie's promise and, tucking the metal cash box under an arm, went on to take care of his remaining chore.

Fred Houk lived on one of the back streets that paralleled Main a block to the north. His clapboard house was tall and narrow, the eaves of the peaked roof dripping with scrollwork. Mrs. Houk opened at Ben Croft's knock and ushered him into the parlor, where her husband sat in an easy chair with the shades drawn, nursing the throbbing pain in his bandaged head. When Croft entered the room, pulling off his sweat-stained hat, the storekeeper looked up, dull-eyed. His lethargy vanished as the sheriff placed the cash box on a table beside Houk's chair.

"You got it!" the merchant exclaimed, and eagerly reached to pull the box toward him; but when he lifted the lid his face fell. "Where's the money?"

Croft reassured him. "The three hundred is locked in my desk. It's evidence, and so is the box; I'll have to hold them until the circuit judge arrives on Wednesday."

"I see. Of course. You have the thief, then?"

Dryly Croft answered, "I have him." Apparently the storekeeper was too miserable with his hurts to care to know more details, once he was sure the money had been recovered. Croft gathered up the cash box. He looked at the other man.

"Pretty rocky?"

Hand to his head, the storekeeper said gruffly, "Doc thinks I'll be all right in a day or two. Guess I came off lucky, everything considered."

"I guess perhaps you did," Croft agreed. "Well, I'll be going. I just figured you'd want to know, right off, that your money was okay." After a few further words he excused himself and left.

He returned to the office and placed the tin box in the desk drawer with the stolen money. Jim Taylor lay unmoving on the cell bunk, hands behind his head and ankles crossed, and stared sullenly at the ceiling; when Croft spoke to him he gave no sign of hearing. The sheriff shrugged and turned to hang up his hat and windbreaker on their nails by the door.

He realized suddenly he had had no breakfast, so he broke out his coffeepot, charged it up and put it on the stove to heat. While he waited he sat at his desk and looked over the mail that had accumulated in the two days he was out of the office. There was nothing of importance. He pushed it aside and sat a moment, rubbing his hands across his face and realizing how dead tired he still was. He would have liked to know how Homer Ingalls was making it, but he figured that would have to wait. The ticking of the alarm clock on a shelf above the desk reminded him that his hour was nearly spent. Bud Taylor could be arriving at any moment.

The coffee started to make noises in the pot. He got up, fetched a couple of heavy china cups. But Jim Taylor just said "Go to hell!" when he was offered a cupful, so Croft poured only for himself. He put the pot on the back of the stove and returned to his chair at the desk. He drank the stuff black, taking his time, and it felt good in his empty belly.

He was swirling the dregs in the bottom of the cup when a noise of arriving horses, pulling to a halt outside his door, warned him he had visitors. He set the cup down. The door flew open then and Bud Taylor's high shape filled the opening.

CHAPTER VI

AT FIFTY-FIVE, an age when most men begin to slack off and admit their best years are behind them, Bud Taylor still had the bull strength and teeming energy of a man twenty years younger. He stormed into the jail office like an angry wind. He looked at the cell where his son had swung up to a sitting position on the edge of the bunk; boots apart and arms akimbo, he came to a stand before Ben Croft's desk and demanded in his arrogant and booming voice, "All right, Croft! Just what is this nonsense?"

Croft looked up into the broad, blunt face, with its intolerant brown eyes and the patchy beard—only faintly sprinkled with gray—that the Diamond T owner never seemed to find time for trimming properly. He quelled his first surge of anger and, placing his hands flat upon the desktop, answered in as calm a voice as he could make it: "Armed robbery and assault isn't nonsense, Bud."

The rancher swore, and swept that argument aside with a movement of his heavy shoulders. He lifted a big hand and pointed a finger at Croft. The finger was yellow with tobacco stain, scarred by a lifetime of toil with ropes and hot irons and wire barbs. "I will give you," Bud Taylor said heavily, "one minute to open up that damned cell and let my boy out of there!"

"No." Croft looked past the finger and into Taylor's angry eyes. He made no move except a shake of the head. "I trailed him from the alley in back of Houk's, clear out to Bishop's place. The three hundred dollars was in his pocket and on the way I picked up the empty cash box from where he'd thrown it away. It's a clear case for Judge Bowen. I'm sorry."

Taylor lowered the hand to his side. He glared at Croft, the thick chest inside his sheepskin coat lifting on angry breathing. Behind him, Mort Keel, the messenger, had slipped in through the doorway and now a new man joined them. This was Taylor's foreman, a seasoned cattleman named Tom Andress and one that Ben Croft respected. He had worked for Diamond T for years and, to him, the brand he worked for came first in everything. He was tall, fined down by saddlework; clean-shaven, with a lantern jaw and a wild shock of grizzled hair and steady blue eyes. He had a sober look on him just now.

Bud Taylor turned to his son, who was standing now holding to the bars of his cage. Jim spoke up quickly. "Hell, there's no use trying to reason with him. No law says I can't ride down an alley. And I don't know anything about any damn cash box."

The rancher looked at him a long moment. Then he turned back and, placing the knuckles of both big hands on the desk, leaned forward to bring his face closer to the sheriff's. His voice was quieter now but it held a sharp edge. "Look, mister! I don't know what you're trying to pull on me, but I don't like it. Come to think of it, I don't even know what you're doing setting there behind that desk. Didn't I send you out to hunt down some missing riding stock?"

The implication that the county sheriff was Taylor's personal errand boy brought a faint warmth into Croft's cheeks, but he swallowed his anger. "We ran into some trouble," he admitted. "My deputy was shot. I had to bring him back."

"And let the bastards have my horses, I suppose?"

"Homer Ingalls' life is more important to me than any bunch of stolen horses," Ben Croft retorted, so sharply that for a moment the big man seemed taken aback. He straightened, stood a moment without speaking while he snapped the fingernails of one hand against the edge of the desk.

"I was sorry to hear about Ingalls," he said gruffly. "He's a good man; I hope he's not too bad hurt. But *you*, mister—I'm telling you! Don't get bullheaded on me, or I'll have that badge off the front of your shirt. And don't think I can't!

"Now, for the last time, you gonna be reasonable, or do you still aim to keep my boy in this stinking jail of yours?"

Ben Croft said, "I don't think I can say it any plainer."

The man's face seemed to close like a fist; his mouth tightened, and he nodded once curtly. "All right!" Without another word he turned and strode from the office, brushing past the two men who stood in the doorway.

Mort Keel flicked Croft with a wicked grin, and then his bold stare went to the prisoner in the cell. "What I tell you, kid? Hang and rattle—you'll be out of this in no time." A final sneer for the sheriff, and he went lunging after his boss.

That left Tom Andress. The foreman lingered, a troubled look on him. He seemed to want to say something, but in the end he gave it up and with a gloomy shake of the head followed the others out, taking the time to close the heavy plank door behind him. Croft heard the three of them walk away, leaving their horses tied in front of the jail. That, he thought, meant they intended to be back.

He let out trapped air from his lungs; for the first time he realized what pressure he'd been under to keep from answering Bud Taylor in kind, turning that ugly scene into something even worse. In the cell, Jim Taylor swore at him.

"You've done it now!" the young fellow growled. "You could have made things a lot easier on the both of us if you'd listened to me in the first place. But no, you had to be muleheaded and drag my pa into this. I *told* you you'd be sorry!"

Croft gave him no answer.

He got his pipe out of the desk, charged it and got it lit. Afterward, picking up a letter that urgently needed answering—a request for information from the sheriff's office in a neighboring county—he tried to concentrate on the words but they tracked before his eyes without really penetrating. He knew Bud Taylor had not been making empty threats. Bud had been nearly speechless with anger, but even so he wouldn't let himself be carried away into statements he couldn't back up. He knew the breadth of his power in this county, and its limitations. He would never have put himself in the position of issuing a warning that he didn't know he could make good.

Ben Croft got out pen and paper and began drafting an answer to his letter, but all the time he worked there at his desk—hearing the wind in the street outside, the ticking of his clock, the snap of pine chunks burning in the stove—he had a feeling he was waiting for a blow to fall; he even found himself curious to see just how Taylor meant to go about bending the law to his will.

Tense nerves jerked at the trample of boots on the sidewalk. Ben Croft laid down his pen, letter unfinished, and looked at the door; suddenly it opened and Taylor and the others were back, and they had someone with them. It was Fred Houk. The storekeeper was bundled up against the autumn day, with a hat set awkwardly on one side of his bandaged head. He looked ill and he stumbled briefly on the threshold, but Bud Taylor's hand clamped under his arm hustled him firmly inside.

Suddenly Croft understood, and his fury had him trembling to think that the rancher would use a sick man to help achieve his purpose. On his feet, he exclaimed, "You had no business dragging this man out of his house, Bud! The doc said—"

"I don't give a damn what the doc said," Bud Taylor answered roughly. "Fred Houk has got a few things to tell us that should clear up this nonsense. Isn't that right, Fred?"

The storekeeper appeared too ill to answer. It was a worried and unhappy-looking Tom Andress who hauled out a chair for him; Houk dropped into it, putting an arm on the desk to steady himself. Standing over him, Bud Taylor said, "All right! Start talking. Straighten this fellow out, Fred."

Croft held himself in with an effort. "I'm listening!"

Fred Houk lifted his head as though it were too heavy for him. He looked at Croft and his eyes slid away. He said, in a lifeless voice, "You arrested the wrong man. It wasn't young Taylor that robbed me. If you'd told me who it was you'd brought in, I could have set you straight right then."

"How?" Croft demanded coldly. "If you never saw the man that hit you?"

"I never saw his *face*," Houk corrected him hastily. "But he was bigger than Jim, and—and he was dressed different." His head turned, as he sought out the man who stood clinging to the cell bars. "This fellow had on denim pants and jacket," Houk said hurriedly. "And a red-checked shirt. . . ."

"You didn't say anything of this before."

"I—I know. My head wasn't too clear. But certainly— whoever it was, it could never have been young Taylor."

Bud Taylor stared boldly at the sheriff, a look of triumph in his eyes. "Well? You satisfied?"

"No!" Leaning, Croft pulled open a drawer, took out a

metal cash box and dropped it on the desk in front of the storekeeper. "This is part of the evidence. Maybe you've forgotten. I showed it to you, and you already identified it as yours!"

The storekeeper's hand, lying on the desk, had begun to tremble. But he shook his head. "I just assumed it was mine. One box looks about like another. But . . . you see, mine had a dent, right here on the side. You see?" He pointed. "And this one don't. So I see now, it ain't mine at all." He tried again to meet Ben Croft's cold stare, but his eyes wouldn't hold. "Sorry," he mumbled. "Anyone can make a mistake, Ben."

Croft knew when he was licked. He drew a breath. "All right," he said, with weary disgust. "You've said enough. I don't know what kind of pressure Bud found to use on you, but I reckon it's for you and your conscience to worry about."

Over by the door, Mort Keel laughed shortly. "Quit grousing, Sheriff. Just go ahead and let the kid out of there."

Croft was already reaching for the keyring. In dead silence he went to the cell, fitted the key and turned it, and flung the metal door wide. Not even looking at the prisoner, he turned to include the lot of them in his savage words: "*All* of you—get out! I've had as much as I can stand in one afternoon! You make me sick to my stomach!"

Bud Taylor's triumphant leer hardened, became ugly. "Go easy, Croft! Don't say nothing you might be sorry for!" But he turned away from the sheriff's stare and, taking Fred Houk by an arm, helped him to his feet. "Come along, Fred. We'll see you home."

"Not so fast!" Jim Taylor, emerging from the cell, was cocky and sure of himself now. He stabbed a thumb in Croft's direction. "This fellow's got three hundred dollars that belongs to me. Now that he knows I never stole it, I want it back."

Holding back his anger with an effort, Ben Croft got the money from the drawer and threw it down on the desk. Young Taylor started to reach for it but instead his father swept it up in one hard fist, saying gruffly, "I'll take care of this!" The look he gave the young man seemed to take Jim aback. Croft saw how Jim tried to stammer something, then clamped his mouth shut, with his good-looking face gone suddenly white as though he had been slapped; it gave the sheriff some small measure of satisfaction.

He had brought out the gun he took from the prisoner; Jim Taylor, without a word, picked it up and shoved it into his pocket. Tom Andress had the door open. He stood aside as Bud Taylor went past him, helping a sick-looking Fred Houk, with Mort Keel laughing and joking loudly as he and Jim Taylor followed them out.

Lingering still, Andress gave Croft a look that was full of embarrassment and shame. Loyalty to his brand wouldn't let the foreman say anything against the man who paid his wages, but his feelings were plain enough.

Ben Croft shook his head. "I don't blame you for this, Tom," he said. "I know you had nothing to do with it."

Tom Andress scowled, and shrugged, and walked out closing the door softly behind him.

CHAPTER VII

BUD TAYLOR kept a place in town, a room above the drug store, with a desk and chairs and file cabinet and an army cot; he used it as an office sometimes or to sleep in when business kept him overnight from the ranch. It was there, returning from seeing Fred Houk to his home, that he found his son waiting, as he had been instructed.

Mort Keel was there, too, lounging indolently in a tilted-back chair with one spurred boot canted up on a corner of the desk. When his boss entered, Keel hastily took his foot off the desk, but the rancher hardly glanced at him. Bud jerked a thumb across his shoulder toward the door. "Out!" he ordered.

The puncher's battered face quickly heated up under the careless contempt in that single word. But men on the payroll did not talk back to Bud Taylor, and Keel swallowed his anger and got up and got out of there, leaving father and son together. The thump of his boots on the stairs was distinct, in the heavy stillness that settled upon his going.

Finally Bud Taylor said, in a tone of blazing scorn, "Well! I hope you're proud of yourself!"

Jim, leaning against an edge of the desk with arms folded, felt the weight of his father's eyes and his own eyes fell before them, to contemplate the toes of his boots. The older man took a quick step nearer and his big hand shot forward, seized his son by the jowls and forced his head up sharply. "You look at me when I'm talking!"

Jim's eyes flashed but he held his tongue, his sullen stare remaining pinned on his father's when the latter had dropped his hand. Bud Taylor shook his head slowly. "I swear, I don't know why I should cover up for you!"

"If that's how you feel," the younger man cried, stung, "then why did you?"

The rancher lifted a warning finger. "Don't raise your voice to me, boy! By God, if it wasn't for your mother I might have just let you take whatever you had coming!" He swung away a step, then turned back and in fury slammed his costly broad-brimmed Stetson down upon the desk. "Do you realize you could have done murder? Just a little extra harder tap with that gun!" His thick chest swelled. "And by God, what I had to do to the poor bastard wasn't too much better! Fred Houk was once by way of being a friend of mine. After today I ain't even going to have his respect—or a hell of a lot left of my own!"

SHERIFF OF SENTINEL

He ran his fingers through a gray-sprinkled thatch of hair as he stared at this son of his in angry bafflement. "You got a tongue in your head? You gonna tell me what could have possessed you to try a damn, stupid thing like this?"

"That's my business."

Taylor's arm swung, the open palm of his hand striking the young man across the face so hard that his head rocked on his shoulders. "Not any longer, you whelp, not since you got *me* dragged into it. Now, don't give me sass. I want the truth. All of it!"

Jim braced himself against the desk. The mark of his father's hand was livid against the bloodless white of his cheek; a tic had appeared beneath one smoldering eye. Then, as his trembling lips tried to form speech, his glance suddenly moved past the older man. And Bud Taylor swung about to face the door.

Covered by the rancher's shouting, the intruder had made his way up the outside steps and into the room before either noticed him. He stood in the doorway, one hand on the knob, an interested glance taking in the scene he had interrupted. He was a man of medium size, rather gaunt of features, with a poor complexion. From his carefully trimmed yellow moustache and his frock coat and string tie and ruffled shirt, anyone familiar with the type would like have guessed—if they hadn't already seen him regularly ensconced at the card tables in Sentinel's saloons for hours on end—that he was one of the tribe of professional gamblers. His name was Gil Ivy.

Bud Taylor, who seldom drank and never played cards for money, had a high intolerance of the breed. His eyes narrowing, he said crisply, "I don't reckon you got any business here, mister."

"I think you're wrong," the gambler said. "About two thousand dollars wrong." He advanced into the room, seemingly not at all bothered by the big man's angry stare, and from a pocket of his figured silk waistcoat dug out a small wad of papers.

"What the hell's that?" Bud Taylor demanded suspiciously.

"Look them over, Mr. Taylor," the gambler said pleasantly. "You'll find they all have your son's signature. They add up to $2,137; I'll settle for an even two thousand. I've been collecting these for a couple of months. Jim finally asked to be given until noon today to raise the money, before I came to see you. That time is up."

Taylor had taken the sheaf of chits and the pair watched as he thumbed through them, reading the sums and the signature. Then he slowly lifted his head and threw a bitter glance at his son. "I can see why you didn't want me to know about this! What have I whelped, anyway?"

Stung, Jim said hotly, "The hell with you! There's no crime in playing a few hands of poker!"

"There should be, if you play this badly!" his father answered dryly. "You dumb, blind idiot! Couldn't you tell you were being suckered? Couldn't you see at a glance just what he is?"

The young man flushed. A corner of Gil Ivy's mouth tightened but otherwise he let no sign of anger ruffle his smooth features. "The use of names doesn't change anything," he pointed out coldly. "I've got two thousand dollars coming to me from someone—I don't too much care who."

Bud Taylor swore. "You ain't got a damn thing coming to you!" he retorted. And without another word he tore the papers across and flung them away.

The gambler stiffened. "For a smart man, that was a stupid trick! You needn't think it will keep me from collecting!"

"No?" the rancher echoed tightly. At something he saw in his eyes, then, Ivy seemed to take warning. He fell back a pace and one hand started toward a pocket of his waistcoat, but by that time Bud Taylor was on him. A hand struck his shoulder, flung him around; a grip fastened itself upon his wrist and wrenched it up into the small of his back as Taylor bulled him toward the door and through it, onto the landing at the head of the steep flight of outside steps.

Bucking and squalling, he tried to break free but he was no match for the big rancher. Between his teeth, Bud Taylor told him, "This is all you'll ever get out of me, you cheap tinhorn!" And without ceremony he simply hurled the other man down the steps.

Ivy had no chance to save himself. He took a bruising tumble, arms and legs thrashing as he spilled helplessly down. When he hit the bottom he lay as one stunned and unable to move, with a streak of blood across his face where it had been laid open against the edge of a step. Bud Taylor stepped back into the office, came out with Ivy's plug hat, which the gambler had lost in the struggle, and scaled it down to him. It struck the man full in the face and seemed to sting him into motion; bawling obscenities, Gil Ivy struggled up onto one elbow and a hand groped toward the pocket of his waistcoat.

"I know you got a stingy gun," Bud Taylor told him with heavy contempt. "Leave it where it is, or I'll come down there and stomp you into the ground!"

Perhaps Ivy didn't trust the gun at that distance, or perhaps his reflexes weren't coordinated well enough just then to use it. He let his hand drop away, empty; but though he only glared back there was a venomous hatred in his eyes that even the rancher couldn't have helped but feel.

Taylor accepted the stare for a long moment, then deliberately turned his back on it. Apparently, as far as the town was concerned, the incident had had no witnesses. Bud Taylor walked back into the office. He looked at his son and saw the latter's sullen expression as a challenge. "Well?" he said.

"He ain't going to let up so easy," the young man said. "He wants his money."

"Let him whistle for it!" his father retorted scornfully. "Gambling debts ain't legally collectible—and if he don't know that, I reckon our worthy sheriff can tell him." The big man sneered faintly as he spoke of Ben Croft. Now he rubbed a palm across his beard and his heavy brows drew into a deeper scowl. "It's you I don't savvy, letting him get his hooks into you. By God, you were a fool!"

"All right!" Jim shouted back, reddening. "So I played a little poker. What else is there to do around here?"

"You lost two thousand dollars, to a man anybody should have pegged for a tinhorn. And then you near broke Fred Houk's skull trying to steal enough for a payoff!"

The young man said bitterly, "I knew damn well I'd get nothing from *you*. Not even sympathy!"

"You knew right! Do you think I ever had time for playing poker? Why, at your age I was already sweatin' out the first herd to wear the Diamond T—the one I parlayed into the biggest spread in all this part of Montana."

"Yeah. And some of your ways of doing it wouldn't bear looking at, any closer than Gil Ivy's card dealing! Don't think I've forgot that blackleg herd you palmed off a few years back. There was about as raw a business as anybody ever heard of. . . ."

Bud Taylor hit him—a meaty smack of knuckles against flesh that sent Jim reeling back against the desk, to carom off it and drop to his hands and knees. The young man crouched there a long minute before he managed to lift his head and look dazedly at his father through the black tangle of hair that had fallen across his forehead.

The rancher stood over him with heavy shoulders rolled forward, his big fist opening and closing to take the sting out of it. A vein pulsed in his temple; his eyes blazed and when he spoke his voice shook with tight, tense fury: "I won't have a whelp like you criticizing my methods, you hear? A man that climbs as high as I have can't always keep his hands too clean. But whatever I did, it was to make the name of Taylor count for something in this world. I wanted the woman I married to have the kind of life I figured she deserved. Yes, and damn it, I wanted—" A long breath swelled his chest. "I wanted something I could pass on one day, to my son!"

From the floor, the young man peered up at him. He hooked a shaky hand over the edge of the desk but remained on his knees, sullen eyes regarding his father as though they had never quite seen him in this light before.

"I don't reckon it ever occurred to you instead," he said slowly, "to let me have some little say about the way things are done *now*."

"You?" his father snapped, and his heavy palm made a scornful, sideways gesture. "Tell me how to run the ranch I built? That ain't likely! Some day, God help me, this brand will pass on to you, and there ain't a damn thing I can do about it; but until I'm dead it ain't gonna happen. I blame your maw for spoiling you rotten. Just the same, when I see what I brung into the world to be my heir I damn near puke with disgust at myself. By God, that's the truth!"

From the look of him there was actually a bad taste in his mouth. He passed a wrist across his lips and, turning his back on his son, he snatched up the hat he'd thrown on the desk. He crossed the room, wrenched open the door and went out slamming it; Jim Taylor, motionless on the floor, listened to the solid thud of his father's boots descending the steps, and after that the stillness was broken only by the young man's harsh, unsteady breathing.

CHAPTER VIII

ON MONDAY, Sheriff Ben Croft walked into the mercantile to find Fred Houk behind the counter, measuring out a sackful of nails for a customer. At sight of the lawman, Houk changed color and his hand shook so that he spilled a patter of nails on the countertop. Murmuring an apology, he finished the job, took payment and made change.

Croft, standing to one side, waited patiently until they were alone. He looked at the storekeeper then, to see that Houk was staring at him and that there was a film of perspiration across the latter's forehead. The bandage had been reduced to a piece of court plaster, fastened over a shaved place on the side of his skull. Houk bobbed his head nervously. "Morning, Sheriff."

Croft said, "Thought I should stop in and see how you're feeling."

"I feel pretty good, I guess." Then the man's face changed and he corrected himself, in a hoarse mumble: "Hell, that's a lie! I feel rotten . . . about that whole business yesterday. I'm sorry, Croft."

"You're sorry?" The lawman eyed him coldly. "What for? You got robbed and slugged; I went out and brought in the wrong man, apparently . . . and let the actual thief get away. Looks like *I* should be apologizing."

Fred Houk looked at the hand lying on the counter in front of him; it was twitching uncontrollably. "For the love of God, Ben! Lay off! You knew all along it was young Taylor that robbed me. How do you think I felt, being forced to lie about it?"

Seeing the man's anguish, the sheriff relented slightly. "All right, Fred. We'll let it go. Still, I'm curious: just what kind of pressure did Bud use on you?"

Houk wagged his head glumly. "It was simple enough: either I'd accept a thousand dollars cash, in settlement for what was stolen and for the knock on the head, or Diamond T would quit buying through my store and begin hauling all its supplies from the railhead at Flynn's Creek. Hell, you know if that was to happen I couldn't even stay in business! Bud Taylor's my main customer!" He spread his hands. "So what could I do but go along? Ain't as though anyone besides me had been hurt, or that anybody stood to gain by me holding out and insisting on the law having its way with that spoiled brat of his."

"It might have done the Taylors some good," Croft pointed out dryly, "for Jim to have to take his medicine—and for Bud to learn there's limits to the power his money gives him." He added, "Was any reason given why the kid tried to pull what he did?"

"I'm as much in the dark about that as you are."

"Likely we never will know." Croft shrugged and pulled away from the counter where he had been leaning. "Well, I guess nobody would want you to cut your throat just to find out—or even to teach the Taylors their lesson."

"Then you do understand my position?" Houk sounded pathetically eager that he should.

"I understand that I'm the goat," Croft answered shortly. "I'm the one has to find a way of explaining why I never managed to catch the crook that slugged and robbed you!" He left the storekeeper to chew on that; too angry to discuss the matter any further, he swung away and walked out through the long, low-ceiling room—and, in the doorway, all but collided with Jane Lawry, who was just entering.

He caught himself in time, stepped back with an apology and a hand reaching for hatbrim. The woman's startled brown eyes lifted to him. "I'm sorry!" he said quickly. "I should look where I'm going!"

"My fault." Dressed for the fall day in a jacket with a dark fur collar that matched her hair, she looked quite stunningly attractive, he decided. He asked, "How's my deputy?"

"Getting restless, I'm afraid, with lying flat on his back." She smiled. "That's a sure sign he's improving. I've tried to help by playing checkers, but he's too good. He always beats me."

Croft said, "Tell him I'll try to drop by this afternoon for a half hour or so, and let him beat *me* for a change."

At that her smile deepened. "Good news for us both," she said with a laugh. Looking at her Ben Croft wondered if she or Homer Ingalls had heard any hint of his trouble with the Taylors; he had said nothing himself, but knowing the ways of rumor he would be surprised if some garbled version of the arrest and release of Jim Taylor wasn't going the rounds. But the woman's pleasant manner gave no hint of such knowledge, and he was just as pleased to have it so. He touched hatbrim to her a second time and left her there, stepping out into the fall morning.

Monday morning was normally a quiet time of week, but with fall roundup in the offing the whole tempo of town and range always picked up. There was more than the usual movement of horses and rigs and foot traffic along the town's streets, and Ben Croft caught a hint of an excitement from it all that he never ceased to feel at this time of year. He knew it for what it was: a nostalgic hangover from the time when he, too, had been in his own small way a cattleman; a time when these first crisp fall mornings had held the busy anticipation of the big event of the season as every outfit, big or small, went onto the range for the market gather. . . .

A familiar-looking buckboard and team had been tied in front of the feed store, next door to Houk's. Warren Bishop, back from the trip that had taken him away from home over the weekend, came out carrying a sack of oats on his shoulder. He was a stocky rancher with graying hair and a strong beak of a nose. He deposited his burden in the rear of the vehicle and went back into the store without appearing to notice Croft. At the same moment the sheriff caught sight of Edie Bishop approaching along the boardwalk.

She walked proudly, yellow head in straw bonnet pertly erect, one hand sweeping her full skirt free of the dirt and litter of the sidewalk, the other carrying a bundle. Croft, his mouth gone a little dry, watched her stop beside the buckboard and place her bundle on the seat. It would be an awkward lift, in her long skirt, up to the high iron step; quickly Croft stepped forward and took her elbow. "Let me help you."

Her reaction was swift, swinging away from him and putting her back to the rig as she jerked her arm free. Her blue eyes met his with a look of such hostility that he dropped his hand. Beneath a gray shawl that was fastened with a brooch, her full young bosom lifted on quickened and angry breathing. She said crisply, "I can manage, thank you!"

Croft could only nod, taken aback. "All right," he said.

Her eyes continued to probe his, more coldly forbidding than he had imagined blue eyes could be. She lashed at him suddenly: "It didn't work, did it?"

He had to pretend he failed to understand her. "What didn't, Edie?"

"Jim's told me what you tried to do yesterday! Honestly, I never thought you could hate a man so much you'd attempt to frame him for a crime you knew he never committed!"

"I did nothing of the sort!"

"How can you stand there and deny it?" she cried indignantly. "Why, you even had that box you tried to claim he'd stolen—as if Mr. Houk wouldn't be able to tell whether it was the right one or not!" She shook her head; her lips, pale with angry emotion, trembled a little. "How *could* you do it, Ben Croft? Are you that jealous of Jim Taylor? Are you that jealous of—of *me?*"

Croft's hands clenched at his sides. Looking down at the girl, he made his grim admission: "Yes, I'm jealous, Edie. I'd be a fool to deny it. And I can only say that business yesterday would look entirely different if I were free to tell the whole story. . . ."

" 'The whole story'?" she echoed, and her voice crackled. "Oh, you're contemptible! You're—" Suddenly feeling overcame her; her right palm came around and cracked smartly against his cheek.

Stung by the blow, Croft's reflexes were still working and almost by instinct he put up a hand and his finger closed upon her wrist. Edie Bishop gasped and tried to jerk free but he held her fast; his cheek smarted to the force of her blow and his spirit seemed numb. He wanted to argue with her, to explain, even as he realized that he had been put in a position where anything he said would sound contrived and unconvincing. Lamely, he managed, "Edie, you got to at least give a man a chance!"

And then he felt a blow on his shoulder that staggered him. The girl broke loose and Ben Croft got his balance and looked around to find Warren Bishop standing beside him. Edie's father had a rope-hardened fist raised and the rancher's face was dark with anger.

"Get away from her, Croft!" Bishop said tightly. "Or by God, I'll break your jaw!"

Edie was pressed back against the side of the buckboard, her eyes wide and a few strands of light yellow hair breaking free of the edges of the straw bonnet. The sheriff got control of himself. He said in a hoarse voice, "I guess I lost my head for a minute. I apologize."

Bishop gave a grunt, as though to say that wasn't good enough. He still wanted to take a poke at the sheriff, obviously, but he seemed to think twice about it and let the fist drop. His eyes, though—blue eyes, very much the color of the girl's—were hard and his voice stony as he said, "After what I heard since I got home, I'm going to tell you just one thing, Croft, and I'll say it just once: you ain't welcome at the Bishop place. I don't think I need to state my reasons." He turned from Croft, then. "Edie," he said roughly, "let's go. . . ."

The sheriff watched him hand the girl up to the seat, where she gathered her bundle into her lap and sat staring straight ahead of her, without another look for Ben Croft. Her father walked around to the other side of the vehicle, got the reins and swung aboard. Croft stepped back as the rancher yelled up his team and slapped the leathers against their rumps, and started the buckboard rolling. Numbed by what had happened, Ben Croft could only watch as it took a corner and passed beyond his sight.

With an effort, then, he shook himself free of emotion and had a look about him, where he stood in the ankle-deep dust by the sidewalk's edge. People who had stopped to watch, out of curiosity, saw the look on his face and began to drift away. Ben Croft took a long breath, and put up a hand and rubbed it across his moustache and mouth and jaw.

It was then that he noticed, in the doorway of the general store, Fred Houk and Jane Lawry watching him. He couldn't see their expressions but a cold chill touched him. Somehow—he couldn't say why—it made the break with Edie Bishop all the more painful and humiliating because the Lawry woman had seen it. . . .

A hand was tugging at his sleeve. He looked down into the face of the youngster, Irwin, and registered what the boy was saying: "Sheriff! Old Charlie, down at the stable, he sent me to look for you."

Ben Croft scowled irritably. "Yes?"

"He didn't say any more than that. He told me you'd know what it was all about."

Suddenly, then, he did understand. "That's right, boy," he said. "Thanks." He was fumbling a dime from his pocket for the youngster, as he turned to gaze downstreet toward the livery stable.

Link Fannin! He had been waiting for the old hostler's word. . . .

Croft had left his gun at the jail and he considered for a moment going after it, then decided no. It wasn't gunplay he had in mind, and there would be less temptation for both of them if he faced the rustler unarmed. But there was no hesitation in him as he stepped to the sidewalk and started down the street; anyone who looked at his face as he passed would have guessed only that the sheriff was absorbed in serious thoughts.

Charlie, the hostler, was at his usual post—in his barrel chair before the stable, where he could bask in the pleasant warmth of autumn sunlight. He cocked a bright eye at the sheriff, jerked his white and shaggy head toward the horses at a saloon tie-pole beyond the barn. "Fannin," he said. "Rode in not five minutes ago."

"How many with him?"

"Couple. That red-headed beanpole Cash Agard, and an-

61

other I didn't know. They tied up and then went across the street with their boss, to the blacksmith's. I heard Link say something about a broke shoe. They're there now."

Croft nodded slowly, his eyes studying the street. "All right, old-timer. Thanks."

"For nothin'!" Charlie grunted. He reached a hand inside his collar to stroke a wrinkled throat. "You ain't thinking to brace the three of them?"

"I'm not that stupid. But there's a few words I figure have to be said, and no better time than now." He touched the old man's shoulder and walked by him, to where the two strange horses were tied before the saloon.

The brands were not familiar; but even Link Fannin would hardly let his men ride into Sentinel on horses stolen from local ranchers. Croft thought it likely they worked in conjunction with longrider outfits who cleaned other ranges and then met to trade their stolen stock. These animals would be the property of ranchers in Wyoming or even farther afield.

Leaning against the tie rail, Croft took out his pipe and set to work digging the dottle from it with his pocketknife. He emptied the bowl by knocking it against the rail, closed the knife and put it away. He started for his tobacco but left it in his pocket, as he saw the three men leave the blacksmith's shed and now come toward him across the dust. Cold and empty pipe in his mouth, Ben Croft stood and waited for them.

Cash Agard, the hatchet-faced one with rust-colored hair hanging nearly to his shoulders, appeared first to notice the sheriff standing near their horses; he ducked his head and apparently spoke a warning that drew the others' attention to him.

Still they came on, with hardly a break in their stride. One was a stranger to Croft, but a definite type of border ruffian and probably a killer. All three were roughly but serviceably dressed in faded jeans, jackboots and coats that had seen considerable hard use. All three wore cartridge belts, with brass filling all the loops and guns in the holsters;

and Link Fannin, in the middle, carried a carbine by its action. Likely he had preferred not to leave it on his saddle while the blacksmith was working on his horse.

As they came toward him Croft kept an eye on the carbine but the rustler continued to let it swing carelessly, its muzzle pointed at the ground. Croft took the pipe from between his teeth and toyed with it, leaning nonchalantly at the end of the tie pole. It should have been instantly apparent that he, for his part, had no kind of weapon on him.

He was sure Link Fannin noticed it. The rustler, with his men flanking him, came to a halt now, boldly confronting the sheriff, a grin showing the wide gap between his two prominent front teeth. Fannin was a man who laughed a lot; he seemed constantly amused at the world around him and the people who followed its rules and lived ordinary lives. It was a laughter edged with contempt, and the intelligent gray eyes held nothing but a chill mockery.

The eyes raked Ben Croft and settled upon the sheriff's face. Boldly pushing, Fannin said, "You looking for me, Sheriff?"

"Should I be?" Croft countered.

The crooked grin widened. "Why, now, that's hardly for me to tell you, is it, Croft?"

Not answering that, Croft pointed the bit of his pipe at the dusty pair of animals drooping in the sun, their reins over the tooth-marked rail. "Yours?"

"Supposing they are?" Fannin suddenly looked a trifle cautious, and the men who flanked him stirred uneasily. The sheriff answered in an indifferent manner.

"I was just observing the brands. They're new to me. Not from around here, anywhere."

Fannin shrugged. "You know how it is. We travel around quite a bit, see a lot of country. We don't always come back forking the same animals we start out on."

"How about the boys who ride with you? Do they sometimes not come back, too?"

It had been a bold thrust and he knew it struck home.

The smile froze at the corners, and in that moment the gray eyes showed a cold hatred. "They don't always," Link Fannin admitted. "Once in a while a man can have an accident—a bad accident."

And that was all he needed to say, to tell Croft who it was had set up the ambush in the pass at Squaw Head, and that the one the sheriff's bullet had reached was dead. Croft said quietly, "Just goes to show it can be dangerous . . . traveling around."

The hating stare met his boldly. Link Fannin waggled the carbine in his hand, letting its muzzle tap against scuffed boot leather. Then his whole expression changed; the eyes turned blank and the lips spread in that meaningless grin of his that covered his true feelings. "Why, sure!" the outlaw said, a chuckle rumbling in his throat. "I'll remember that, Sheriff."

He pivoted on one boot sole, starting to swing wide around Croft and the hitch pole; his men, moving to accompany him, halted in their tracks as Ben Croft spoke curtly: "Something else to remember, Fannin: I can't close this town or this county to you, because I've got no grounds —none that the law will let me act on. But I'll tell you now that if I ever catch you or any of your men with a cow bearing a Sentinel County brand, then you had just better damn well have a bill of sale you can show me. Now, go chew on that a while!"

The two men—the grinning outlaw and the blunt and forthright lawman—faced each other with that threat and challenge hanging between them in the crisp morning stillness. It was Fannin who broke gaze, though he did it with a bark of scornful laughter. He walked on, his men at his heels; pivoting where he stood, Ben Croft kept them in sight as they stepped up onto the plank walk and crossed it to shoulder their way through the door of the saloon. He saw a few bystanders eyeing him, saw the looks of fright on one or two who seemed to understand the meaning of what had been happening in front of them.

He shrugged and scowled, then shoved the clay pipe

savagely into his pocket. His hand, he discovered, was trembling; partly from fear, he admitted, but mostly from a numbing frustration.

A man could feel like that when no step he took, in any direction, seemed to get him anywhere. Fannin, Edie Bishop, the Taylors: no matter where he turned he found himself facing yet another blind, blank wall. He wondered, just a little grimly, when things were going to start breaking his way for a change. . . .

CHAPTER IX

THE PERIOD just before fall gather was the cattle country's busiest time, with a hundred final chores that demanded attention. There was saddle stock to be checked and re-shod, gear to be carefully examined and repaired—a man's life could hang, in moments of crisis, by a frayed strand in his saddle rope or a worn cinch strap. Meanwhile chuck wagons and work rigs had to be got ready, and the shelves of every town merchant risked depletion as ranch after ranch sent in to pick up supplies.

Later, for the three weeks that the crews were in the field, Sentinel would lie somnolent and nearly deserted; but now there was life enough, and a mounting anticipation that would reach its climax on the final Saturday night. That night the town would see a blowout, with an annual roundup dance on the second floor of the courthouse, and all three of the town's saloons going full blast before the onset of hard and unbroken labor.

For the sheriff, roundup meant an uncertain period of sticking close to his office, never knowing when a call for help might come in. Tired men's tempers flared sometimes; a dispute over the reading of a brand could lead to arguments in which men had been hurt and even killed. Ben Croft knew he must hold himself in readiness, at any hour of day or night, to answer a summons that might never come at all.

On Saturday morning he walked over to Jane Lawry's for a few minutes with his deputy. Homer Ingalls was improving mightily under the fine care he was receiving. A week after being wounded, he was out of bed and able to get around some by using the cane Croft had bought him. He insisted on demonstrating, hauling himself out of his easy chair and making a tour of the living room, leaning on the stick and letting only the faintest tightening of the muscles of his cheeks betray the effort it cost him. "I shouldn't be setting around here!" he insisted for the twentieth time. "I ought to be back at work."

"You're doing fine," Croft told him. "Come Monday, we'll see. I'd say you need a couple more days."

Homer snorted in disagreement. "I'm thinking about tonight!"

"I'll make out."

Despite his deputy's protests, Croft noticed that he seemed glad enough to settle back into the chair again, with an explosion of breath that fluttered his lips. He laid the cane on the floor beside him. "What about Fannin? Any more sign of him? Or do you figure you scared him out of Sentinel for good?"

"Of course I never scared him out! He wouldn't let *me* keep him away."

"Could be trouble if he was to show up today, of all times. . . ."

"Why should he? He knows the crews will be in and likkering up. No point in riding into a hornet's nest, just to prove he's not afraid of anyone. . . . The world knows that already! Fannin's not the kind to risk his neck unless it pays off in hard cash!"

Homer Ingalls considered this, and had to agree. "So

he'll be biding his time, but not for too long. He can only keep that gang of his together by using it. I wager that if he's still around he'll find a way to use it before roundup's over. . . ."

They dropped the subject of Link Fannin, then, as Jane Lawry came into the living room on her way upstairs with an armful of freshly ironed sheets. She smiled with evident pleasure at sight of the sheriff; the latter came up off the sofa, picking his hat from his boottoe where he had hung it, and they exchanged a few words about the weather. It was when she started to turn away, on her errand, that Ben Croft took a sudden awkward step forward.

"Jane? Mrs. Lawry?"

She looked at him, her head tilted a little on one side, a question in her eyes. She smoothed a spotless sheet with an absent movement of a hand. "Yes?"

"Uh, it just occurred to me," he stammered, while Homer Ingalls watched them in open and disconcerting interest. "Are you going to the dance tonight?"

"I wasn't planning on it. No."

"Would you consider going with me?"

Her expression changed subtly. He had not known what reaction to expect, but he wasn't prepared for the frown that puckered the space between her brows and erased the smile from her mouth. She looked at him like that for a long moment before she answered, with a trace of coldness, "I'm afraid not, Mr. Croft."

"No?" Taken aback, he blinked and heard himself stammering. "Any particular reason?"

"If you must hear it," she answered, stiffly, "it happens I'm well aware that I'm your second choice. If you thought there was any hope of Miss Edie Bishop being in a mood to go with you, it would never have entered your head to ask me instead." Her brown eyes flashed. "And I'm just enough of a female to resent that, Mr. Croft!"

He stared at her for a long moment, seeing the angry hurt in her eyes, before his own stubborn anger began to rise in him. He moved his shoulders and, scowling a little, said bluntly, "Well, that was honest at any rate! Forget I asked. I'll try not to embarrass you that way again!"

Croft nodded stiffly and was about to turn away when a word from Homer Ingalls halted him. "Hold on, Ben!" Turning to the woman, the old deputy said sharply, "This ain't my mix, but damned if I like to see two friends of mine get off on the wrong foot! Would it make any difference to you, Jane, if I told you I know for a fact Ben Croft never before asked *any* woman to a dance—as long at least as I've known him? And by that I mean the Bishop gal, or anybody!"

Jane Lawry's frown changed, became a look of perplexity that she turned on Croft, searching for enlightenment. "What is he telling me, Ben?"

Warmth began to work through the sheriff's cheeks. Gruffly he said, "Just that I'm the world's worst dancer! Naturally clumsy, I guess. I go to these things to stand on the sidelines, and watch the ones who can do it." He hesitated, then blurted the rest of it: "But seems to me it's wrong for someone like you to go on burying yourself in this boardinghouse, never getting out of it, never having any fun. It's high time you had a change. And so I was thinking, if you'd have let me take you tonight, that there'd be men on hand who'd be more than glad to see that you had plenty of partners to dance with. So you see, you wouldn't really have to be stuck with me. . . ."

She stared at him, and slowly her eyes filled with tears. "Oh, Ben, I'm sorry! I didn't understand! You made the offer only on my account . . . and then I had to say those horrible things! Can you ever forgive me?"

"Will you let me take you?" he countered.

"But of course!" she said, smiling. "I'd love to go. And I just bet you're not such a terrible dancer, either!" And seeing Ben Croft's answering smile, softening the craggy lines of his face, Homer Ingalls gave a grunt of satisfaction.

It was Sentinel's big night, and the town began to fill up long before the early dusk fell. Rigs and saddled horses lined the streets and filled the vacant lot next to the courthouse. Ben Croft knew from past experience that the chances were he would have some work to do tonight; even though he was a county officer, not paid to keep order in town. But there was no constable or town marshal to jail common cowhands who happened to take on more whiskey than they could handle, and he often had to do the duties of one. But this would come much later in the evening, as he explained to Jane Lawry; chances were that nothing would come up to call him out this early.

They walked the few blocks from the boardinghouse, Jane having refused to hear his suggestion of hiring a buggy for such a short distance. Things were already started and light spilled from every window of the big hall above the courtroom; as they mounted the stairs they could hear the thump of drum and squawl of cornet and whine of concertina, and a busy hum of voices. They entered a scene of movement and sound, beneath the glow from paper lanterns and the sweep of colored streamers that festooned the walls and ceiling.

Croft checked their wraps and returned the greetings of men that he knew. He looked over the stag line, the people grouped around the refreshment tables, and the couples circling the waxed floor; when he turned again to the woman beside him, and found her brown eyes studying him, he somehow knew she guessed who he was looking for. But there was no sign, as yet at least, of Edie Bishop's bright beauty.

If she did know what was on his mind, Jane made no mention of it. Instead she indicated the musicians' platform and said, smiling, "They're playing a waltz. You know how to waltz, don't you?"

"I guess, after a fashion."

"There's nothing in the world easier. I'm a little rusty myself, but I'll take a chance if you will." And she smiled encouragement as she lifted her arms to him. Croft gingerly took hold of her. With her fingers resting lightly on his sleeve, he hesitated to pick up the beat, saw an opening in the flow of traffic and plunged her into it.

Actually things went much better than he could have expected. Though Croft was sweating with concentration and the dread of making a fool of himself, Jane Lawry fitted lightly in his arms and seemed able to avoid his clumsy boots, smiling encouragement when she caught his eye. He almost began to enjoy himself. The musicians went directly into a second waltz and he went with them, swinging across the floor with an abandon that was quite unusual for him. Apparently, Jane Lawry was the kind of partner who made a man seem to dance better than he really could.

Then he saw Edie Bishop go by, in the arms of young Jim Taylor.

Croft had actually forgotten to watch for them and didn't notice when they entered the hall. Now as he caught sight of them, and saw the angry scowl Taylor gave him above Edie's bright head, he missed a step and forced Jane to collide with another couple; this completely unnerved him. When, a moment later, the band started in on "Buffalo Gals" he begged off and led his partner instead to the rear of the room, to get her a glass of punch at the refreshment table.

"I'm sorry," he grunted. "I told you I was clumsy."

"You're doing just fine," she insisted.

She really seemed to be having a good time, he thought; her face was warm and her eyes sparkling. She looked very attractive this evening, in a simple gray skirt and shirtwaist, with a cameo at her throat and her hair clubbed behind her neck with a bit of ribbon. Croft noticed the admiring glances she received, from men who had likely never given more than a moment's thought to Tom Lawry's widow—thinking of her simply as a woman who ran a boardinghouse, without stopping to notice how young and handsome she really was.

It made him happy to know that he had judged right, in insisting that she break free of the restricting cage she'd forced herself to live in since her husband's death.

"Buffalo Gals" had been put through its paces and after an interval the music started again—another waltz this time. Croft felt the woman's touch upon his sleeve, saw her motion with a nod of her head. "Now's your chance," she told him.

Looking, he saw that Taylor had disappeared somewhere for the moment and that Edie stood alone, gazing about her in a way that suggested she wanted someone to come and invite her to dance. "She can't do any more than refuse," Jane Lawry urged; but Croft, remembering the last time he had spoken to her—her anger and the humiliation of her hand striking his face—grimly shook his head.

Then Paul Rogers, owner of Sentinel's hotel, was there to exchange a greeting and ask Jane for the dance. Her glance asked Croft's permission and he said gruffly, "Sure, why not?" After all, it was his purpose in bringing her—to let her have a good time and mingle with people. Yet as she swung away in Rogers' arms—saying over her shoulder, "We'll waltz another set later, Ben"—he was surprised to experience what he could only define as a pang of jealousy. And that, of course, was simply foolish.

Alone, he looked again for Edie but saw her moving onto the floor with a rancher from Trout Creek. Just as well, he thought glumly. And finding himself for the moment at loose ends, he got his hat and jacket from the desk and went downstairs to have a look at the evening.

Things seemed quiet enough, despite the influx of people and the air of celebration that always dominated the town on Saturday night before roundup. Standing under the big cottonwood that dropped its leaves in a silent rain over sidewalk and vacant lot by the courthouse, Ben Croft leaned his shoulders against the trunk and got out his pipe and can of shag. Oddly, he found his thoughts were on Jane Lawry as he filled the bowl and tamped it with a broad thumb, took a kitchen match from his shirt pocket.

He was about to snap the match alight when a sound reached him.

It was the crackling of dead leaves beneath a cautious

71

footstep, close beside him. Head turning sharply, he peered and thought he saw a darker shape against the night. The man, if it was one, had gone motionless as though aware that the sound betrayed him. Light from the windows of the hall, on the second story, did not reach to this spot and Croft could not be certain whether he saw or only imagined the dim oval of a face. He lowered pipe and unlit match and demanded, "Who's there?"

"Croft?" a voice answered from the shadows. "You son of a bitch! I figured that was you!"

The sheriff let a slow breath out between his lips. Straightening from his lean against the cottonwood trunk, he let the match drop and fumbled at the flap of his jacket pocket, quietly stuffing away the pipe. "All right, Jim," he said. "What do you want?"

"What do you think I want, damn you?" Jim Taylor came toward him now, melting from the denser shadow. His voice was harsh and sounded a little wild to Croft. "There's rumors all over the place about you having the nerve to try and arrest me for robbery last week. You got half the town laughing at me!"

"The half that isn't laughing," Croft retorted roughly, "has likely guessed you were guilty, and also knows how it was you got off!"

Young Taylor mouthed an obscenity. He was close enough now that his breath touched Croft's face and the sheriff caught a whiff of raw alcohol; he supposed young Taylor had left the dance for the purpose of sampling something stronger than the fruit punch they served upstairs. Ben Croft said, "If you're thinking of talking up a fight with me, remember I already licked you once. Use your head and go back upstairs and forget this!"

With a strangled yell, the man charged him.

Croft had known it was coming, and he stepped away from the wild right swing he had figured would be reaching for his head. His own left fist shot straight out and Taylor ran into it, and he felt flesh mash against bone and heard a gasp of pain as the other was halted in his tracks. "Jim," he started to say, in a last effort to persuade him. "Don't be a fool!"

And then his words choked off as, without warning, an arm clamped about his neck from behind, forcing his head back and choking off his wind; a hand trapped his right arm at the elbow and yanked it savagely behind him. A voice, directly in his ear—he was sure it was Mort Keel's—grunted in heavy triumph: "I got him for you, kid! Go ahead, beat the whey out of him!"

Half strangled, helpless with the crook of Keel's elbow clamped like iron about his throat and forcing his head back, Ben Croft reached desperately with his one free hand but his fingers only clawed at the material of Keel's canvas coat, unable to find purchase. The roar of his own blood sang in his ears. And now Jim Taylor was coming at him, making choked sounds of eagerness and fury, and Croft knew he was in for it.

If the light had been stronger it would have been worse. Taylor came in swinging both fists wildly, trying to deal punishment; but his first blow, aimed at Croft's face, struck Keel's arm instead and drew an angry grunt from him. The second drove into the sheriff's middle, but Croft had tightened his muscles against it. Though it hurt, it didn't sink deep into his wind. Unable to protect himself, he brought one boot forward, then, in a hard kick. It landed solidly, and from the shout that broke from young Taylor he thought he had taken him on the kneecap. Jim stumbled backward.

And Ben Croft dropped abruptly to his knees. He thought his neck would break, but the suddenly limp weight of his body pulled Mort Keel down with him. Kneeling, Croft bent sharply forward and his left hand, clamping down on the collar of the man's windbreaker, jerked hard. Thrown off balance, Keel's own weight carried him over Croft in a clumsy forward somersault. He lost his hold on Croft's right arm and his throatlock was broken.

Dazed, Ben Croft shook his head as he crouched there, gasping for breath. He raised his head, then, and saw that

Mort Keel had been flung clear of the deeper shadows. He was scrambling around there, rolling to his knees; a vagrant ray of lamplight from a window caught the glint of steel as he pulled his belt gun.

Croft hurled himself forward. He knew Keel was a man of unpredictable temper, especially when drinking, and he couldn't guess what might happen if that gun got loose. He struck hard and they both went down, but Croft missed his grab for the other's gunwrist. His own weight pinning the man under him, he made a wild grab and this time his hand closed over Keel's fingers.

The gun went off, the jolt of the explosion shocking Croft's arm from wrist to elbow; muzzle flash tore open the darkness and he saw the gleam of Keel's eyeballs, and the teeth behind his pulled-back grimace. A fist struck glancingly along Croft's cheekbone like a firebrand, but he kept his grip on that other hand and now he slammed it against the ground. The gun went off a second time—it must have been on a hair trigger. The sound of the two shots mingled; around them, tied horses snorted and stomped in terror.

He slammed the wrist against the ground a second time; Keel's fingers opened and the gun slipped out of them. Instantly Croft pulled back and drove his fist into the man's face, and felt him go motionless amid the rustling carpet of fallen leaves.

That left young Taylor, who had started the trouble. Croft climbed to his feet and, looking for him, found the man kneeling a little distance away, nursing his crippled kneecap and staring as though dazed by the gunshots. As Croft started toward him, Taylor straightened and gave ground, limping. He backed against the side of a parked wagon; there, full in the spill of window light, he lifted his fists.

Ben Croft, carried forward by hot anger, simply batted his arms aside and gathered a fistful of the man's coatfront in a hard grip, his own right fist cocked to strike; but when he saw that the other was past effective fighting he

74

gave a grunt and let him fall back against the wagon box, his own furious anger quickly cooling.

He scrubbed a hand across his thick moustache and said, in a tone of utter contempt, "If I couldn't get even with a man without arranging it with someone else to jump him for me, I'd be big enough to forget about it!"

He turned away then, as he became aware of other people gathering out of the autumn night. It was the gunfire that brought them, of course. Now others, men and women both, were pouring from the doorway at the foot of the stairs leading from the dance floor. Excited questions gradually silenced as Bud Taylor shoved his way forward.

The rancher demanded, in his heavy and carrying voice, "What's going on here, Croft? What were those gunshots?" And then Taylor caught sight of his own son, half crouching against the wagon box, and he stopped in his tracks as though he had walked into a wall.

Croft looked at him. "I'm not going to answer you, Bud," he said coldly. "You can ask this pair, if you think they'll tell you. But keep them away from me tonight if you don't want them jailed! I mean it!"

Mort Keel was up on one elbow, feeling his jaw as though it might have come unsprung. Croft showed a trickle of blood on his cheek. This, and Jim Taylor's torn and rumpled clothing, ought to have been evidence enough to let anyone know there had been a fight . . . and give them a good guess who had been the winner. Scowling, Bud Taylor looked at his son, but the latter wouldn't meet his eye. And now Ben Croft picked up his hat and, walking over to the fallen Keel, leaned for the gun that lay among the drift of crackling leaves. Returning, he offered it to Bud Taylor, butt first. "That belongs to Mort," he said coldly. "Don't give it back to him till he's sober enough to leave it in his holster!"

Taylor looked at the gun, then slowly put out a hand for it and dropped it into a pocket of his coat. He stood aside as Croft pushed by him without another word and, pulling on his hat, headed toward the group in the doorway.

A lantern burning above the door put its spray of yellow light over the group clustered there, silently staring at him, and the first faces he saw were those of Warren Bishop and his daughter. He saw Edie's look of distaste and horror, and the way she drew back, almost as though she were loath to have her skirt brush against him. He paused and gave her a long look, then moved on without trying to speak to her. He passed on to where Jane Lawry stood by herself, hugging her elbows as the chill of the night struck through the material of her shirtwaist. Croft stopped before her and said, gruffly, "I'm sorry. That wasn't anything I planned!"

Her eyes, filled with concern, searched his face. "You're hurt!"

Touching his cheek, Croft found blood where a slugging blow had split the skin. He nodded. "I better go over to the office and clean myself up some."

"Can I help you?"

"No," he told her gruffly. The crowd was breaking up, drifting away or turning back into the hall as they saw there was to be no more excitement. Curious eyes still raked Croft's face but he paid them no attention. Yonder, Bud Taylor had his son and Mort Keel engaged in low-voiced conversation; Croft could feel the animosity beating in his direction from the three of them.

"It's cold out here," Croft said. "You better get inside."

"Do you think there might be more trouble?"

"Bud's not apt to let those two get out of hand again. After I've washed up I want to take a look around town, see how things are going. I'll be around to pick you up in an hour—that is, if you think you'll be ready to go home by then." He added, "I warned you what it might be like, going out with me."

"Don't worry about that," she said, and smiled. "Remember, we're going to waltz another set before we go home."

"Whatever you say." An answering smile broke the bleak line of his mouth. As he watched her turn back inside the building, he found himself wondering just what there was about this woman that made him feel easier and somehow more on friendly terms with a disappointing world.

CHAPTER X

JIM TAYLOR suddenly had his hands full. In this brush-choked draw, right up in the pine- and rock-studded hills that marked the northern limits of his father's range, he had suddenly and without warning jumped a big old steer, a tough four-year-old that had somehow eluded earlier roundup crews and gone wild. He was a wily, independent animal who knew this chopped-up bit of country and was determined not to be cut out of it. But the brand on his hide was Bud Taylor's Diamond T, and he carried Taylor's right crop earmark, and Jim went grimly after him.

He had a good, trained cowpony under him and he could handle a rope well, but that old steer was a tough problem. The first good cast Jim got at him, he shook the loop off his horns just as it seemed about to settle and, switching directions in midstride, took off at a right angle that nearly caused Jim's horse to spill and pile up under him. The pony pulled out of that, but the steer was already dodging into a thicket of scrub pine where there was no chance of using a rope. Doggedly, young Taylor stayed with him.

Pine branches whipped at him, plucked the hat off his head, gave him one stinging scrape across cheek and temple that caught a corner of his eye and blinded him with quick tears. Finally he had to haul in, pawing at his vision to clear it. He saw the red hide of that outlaw steer vanishing into thicker growth and, swearing with frustration, dragged out his belt gun and threw a shot after it.

The bullet missed; the steer ran on and was gone. But the battering echoes of the shot, quickly blotted up by the timber, had an effect on young Taylor. It had been purely stupid to try to vent his fury in killing an animal that was worth money to his father. Awareness of what Bud Taylor would have had to say, if he knew, helped to settle him.

He swore again, in weary disgust. Afterward, while the pony got its wind back, he took his time hauling in the rope and coiling it. He used his neck cloth to dab at his smarting eye.

He seemed to be constantly in a foul mood that nothing in the past two and a half weeks of roundup had done anything to ease. Relations with his father had never been worse; Bud Taylor's contempt for his son had deepened to sheer disgust after that incident at the dance in town; if he wasn't man enough to settle his grievances with Ben Croft, not even when he had Mort Keel to help him, then Bud could see no hope at all for him. He had scarcely spared a word for his son since.

In a last desperate attempt at self-assertion, Jim Taylor had demanded he be put in charge of one of the two Taylor roundup wagons—or if not that, at least be sent to rep for Diamond T with one of the other outfits. Bud, dismissing this out of hand, had ordered him to report out with one of the wagon crews. And to Jim this was the final humiliation.

Apparently there was no way out of the box he was in. Looked like he could spend the rest of his life trying to prove himself, without ever denting Bud's contempt for him. . . .

He sawed the reins with an angry jerk as he turned back to find his hat, where the tree limb had raked it off. It took a moment's searching; locating it, he swung down and picked up the hat, knocked dirt from it against his leg and punched some shape into it. He was standing there by his pony when he glanced up, suddenly, at the sound of a rider working toward him through the trees.

When the man reined to a halt, young Taylor could

only stare at him with an astonishment that quickly shaded into suspicion. "What the hell are you doing here?" he demanded.

"A saddle isn't exactly a home to me," Gil Ivy admitted. The gambler's lips quirked crookedly beneath the trimmed yellow moustache; even he was amused at the picture he made in his broadcloth town suit and plug hat, out here so far removed from his regular haunts of saloon and gambling hall. "As it happens," he said, "I was looking for you, friend."

"My pa ran you out of this country!"

The raddled cheeks drew tight; the gambler's black eyes narrowed down with remembered anger. "He kicked me down a flight of stairs," Gil Ivy corrected him, "and it's something I promise he'll regret!" He pinned the younger man with his stare. "You didn't really think I'd give him the satisfaction of thinking I was that easily got rid of?"

"You've made yourself pretty scarce since it happened."

"I've been around—and for good reason. In case you'd forgotten, you're still into me for two thousand dollars."

"You can go whistle for it," the young man said, with a shrug. "Pa convinced me I was a damn fool to think there was any way you could force me to pay it."

He pulled on the hat and then froze, hand still raised, as he heard the whisper of metal against cloth and saw the stubby derringer pointed at his face. In spite of himself he felt his skin go cold and his throat suddenly dry out. He looked at the face above the gun and finding his voice he exclaimed, "You don't suppose I'd have it *on* me!"

"No. But you're going to get it for me," Gil Ivy told him. "I've been watching for a chance to pick you up, alone. Now, get in that saddle. . . . There's somebody wants to talk to you."

"Who?" the young fellow demanded sharply. But the gambler shook his head.

"You'll find out soon enough." He gestured with the ugly little gun. "I'm not a patient man. Do as you're told."

And he watched as, reluctantly, the other moved to find the stirrup.

A vagrant whiff of woodsmoke alerted Taylor, and minutes later his horse threaded between a pair of granite boulders and dropped down through a screen of lodgepole and aspen, into the well-grassed glade where half a dozen men had made temporary camp. Their horses, under saddle, moved about pulling at the grass.

The smoke Jim Taylor had noticed rose in a blue column, twisting lazily above the snapping flames of a tiny fire. A blackened coffeepot sat aslant among the burning pine sticks, and now Taylor caught that odor too and it caused the glands in his throat to salivate with a pleasant aching. The men of this camp had broken off their activities to watch the newcomers ride down into the clearing. Taylor was nervously aware of the cold and expressionless looks he got, but he mostly gave them little attention; he had already caught sight of a face that he recognized, and it filled him with a heart-quickening fear.

This man stood alone, tin cup in hand, shoulder against a treetrunk and a carbine leaning close beside his knee. Link Fannin pushed away from the tree now and stepped forward, a grin shaping up on his wide mouth as he looked at Gil Ivy. "So you got him."

"He didn't want to come very much," the gambler said. "I persuaded him, though."

Fannin turned to the prisoner. "Get down."

Scared as he was, as he looked around at the evil faces, Jim Taylor nearly balked. But he saw the wink of sunlight on the derringer held carelessly in Gil Ivy's hand; scowling, trying to stiffen the tremor from his limbs, he stepped out of saddle.

He shook his head stubbornly when Link Fannin indicated the coffeepot. "No thanks! I'm particular who I drink with—even coffee! I've got no business with this bunch of longriders!"

"Oh, I think you do." Link Fannin looked amused rather

than angry. Unruffled, sipping at his own cup, he said, "For openers, there's the two thousand you owe Gil Ivy. He's asked me to collect it for him."

"He knows that's ridiculous! I haven't got five bucks in my pocket!" But next moment young Taylor thought he saw the shape of the outlaw's thinking, and in spite of his fear he had to let out a bark of laughter. "*Ransom!*" He looked at Fannin with contempt. "Good God! If *that's* what's on your mind, I'll tell you now you can forget it! The old man would never pay, not if you killed me. Instead he'd run down the lot of you and settle with you, for the nerve of trying to hold him up. You'll dig your own grave—I promise you!"

Fannin looked at him above the rim of the tin cup, and after a moment he nodded. "Kind of how I figured," he said. "Kidnapping is a sucker's game. No, Bud Taylor won't pay us a penny—and you can't. All the same, I think we got a way figured to get Gil his money, and a bit extra for the rest of us. And you're the one who's going to do it."

"Me?"

The outlaw continued pleasantly, as the younger man stared. "Gil Ivy's a chap who knows how to find out about things, keeping his ears open, asking the right questions of the right people. And he's been learning some things about your pa's business deals. Go ahead, Gil. *You* tell him."

"What I heard," the gambler said, "is that even though roundup isn't over, a crew under Tom Andress put a Diamond T herd on the trail yesterday morning for the loading pens at Flynn's Creek. A big shipment—eight hundred head, I understand. The buyer's a man named Denton."

Scowling, Jim Taylor nodded. "Pa does a lot of business with Ed Denton. . . ."

"Right. And the way I hear it, the K.C. market is in such good shape just now that this man is anxious to take advantage of it: he's paying a top price for immediate delivery."

"You listen pretty good," young Taylor conceded shortly. "But you haven't said what this has got to do with me."

Link Fannin tossed his empty cup beside the fire. "Does Denton know you, personally?"

"Sure. I been along a couple of other times when Pa made beef deliveries to him."

"How come you weren't picked to go with this one?"

He shrugged. "How the hell would I know?"

Fannin nodded as though with satisfaction. He dug into a pocket of his jumper, brought out a plug of tobacco and a clasp knife. "All right, kid, I'll tell you what's going to happen. The bunch of us ·takes us a little ride over to Flynn's Creek. We can get there, easy, before Andress and the crew have got their cattle loaded. Then, when it's time for the payoff, *you* step in and collect from this fellow Denton."

The young man blinked. He watched the other pare off a chunk of tobacco against a callused thumb, and transfer it to his mouth. He blurted, "What makes you think he'd give me the money?"

"Why the hell not? You said he knows you. Anybody with the name of Taylor should outrank a mere foreman."

"And Tom, I suppose, is just going to stand by with his teeth in his mouth?"

"Well, now," the rustler said, grinning around the lump of tobacco distending his dark cheek; he made a circle with the point of his knife, indicating the men of his crew. "That's why we're gonna be on hand: to see Tom Andress keeps his mouth shut!"

"Ain't hard to see what's really chewing on you," he went on before young Taylor could interrupt. "You're wondering what *you* get out of this—it's only natural. Well, let me tell you, kid, nobody wants to be greedy. After all, you'll be doing the work. So, once you collect, Gil Ivy will take the two thousand you owe him; then we split the rest, right down the middle. Eight hundred head, at forty per—figure it out. A half for you!"

The protest Jim Taylor had started died on his tongue; for the first time he felt a faint stirring of interest. But he shook his head, saying roughly, "Hell, man! If I do this and Pa ever gets his hands on me, he'll kill me sure! I'd have to leave the country!"

Gil Ivy spoke quietly. "Aren't you the one used to tell me how bad you hate this Montana? How it gravels you to be under the old man's thumb, without even spending money, and no say at all in the way things are done? If you really meant half the things you said about wanting to get away, here's a chance the likes of which you might never see again. You better think about it!"

Suddenly he *was* thinking about it.

Fifteen thousand dollars! He figured it a second time and it still came out the same—a sudden, glittering prize, and so tempting that any normal instinct for caution was swamped. He forgot to wonder if these men were capable of keeping their word, whether they actually intended to let him pocket half of all that money. Resentments against his father and against the frustrations of his life blinded him to other things, as he thought he saw the solution to all his galling frustrations and needs. And it would not be stealing, but merely a collection of some part of his rightful share in his father's wealth.

His mind made up, he drew a slow breath. "I tell you what," he said. "There's someone I have to talk to first, someone I can't leave this country without. But if she says she'll go with me, then it's a deal. I'm in it, for the whole distance!"

"Go away with you, Jim?" A frown of perplexity tugged at Edie Bishop's clear brow and clouded her beautiful eyes. "Right now, just like this?"

"If you love me, you will!" he persisted. "I tell you, I can't stand it around this place any more! There's nothing for me here!"

"Why, there's everything! The ranch, your parents . . ."

"Pa is a hard-nosed tightwad who wants nothing from me but to make my life unbearable! I know damn well he's going to live forever—and I'll never be anything but one of the hired hands, who has to go to him begging any time

I want a penny to spend! Well, that's just not good enough! I want to live my own life; I want to be free. And I'm giving you the same chance."

"Jim, I—I don't know!" she exclaimed, close to tears in the overwhelming confusion of the choice he had sprung upon her without warning. "At least give me time to think. . . ."

Quickly moving closer, he caught her by both arms. "There *isn't* any time! It's got to be now! You don't like it here any better than I do." An impatient gesture with his head indicated the stretch of rangeland beyond the kitchen window, the blue line of piny mountains. "You always agreed that you wanted to escape. You wanted to see a real city for once, like San Francisco. Have you forgotten?"

Her eyes searched his. The tip of a pink tongue wet her lips. "Is *that* where you're going—to San Francisco? Honestly, Jim?"

"As straight as an arrow," he assured her. "We'll be married there. We'll have money, and the world at our feet. No more dust and wind and blizzard. No more of *that!*" He pointed to the pile of washing on the table, the sadirons heating on the stove.

"But . . . what in the world will I tell Papa?"

"You'll tell him nothing! If he had any inkling of this he'd move heaven and hell to stop us. You know that. Of course, once you're legally my wife there's nothing he can do about it; but until then we've got to be very careful. It comes to this: do you really love me? Do you trust me enough?"

Her blue eyes searched his face. Then she slowly nodded; she swallowed and said, "What do you want me to do?"

Jim Taylor somehow kept the triumph and the surge of relief from showing in his face; if she had flatly refused, he didn't know what he could have done about it. He said quickly, "You go and pack. Whatever you really need to take, try to get it into one suitcase. Meanwhile I'll saddle you a horse. Without pushing too hard we should make

Flynn's Creek by tomorrow morning. I'll get you a room at the hotel, and you can rest while I'm taking care of some business that will give us the money we need. Later we'll board the train for California. . . ."

He could feel her trembling, knew that she was frightened. He pulled her close and kissed her; her hands came up and clutched at him. Releasing her he looked down into her pale and anxious face. "You sure you're game?"

"If *you're* sure you love me. . . ."

Taylor gave her his most reassuring smile, and squeezed her shoulder. But when he went out to the barn he left the girl staring after him, wringing her hands in a torment of anxiety.

CHAPTER XI

HOMER INGALLS came into the sheriff's office, where Ben Croft was at his desk, using an idle afternoon to clean out ancient correspondence and get rid of outdated stuff that merely took up room. Homer was getting around well enough these first few days since his return to duty, though he tended to walk with a slight sideward warp, favoring newly-mended tissues.

He hung his hat and coat on a nail, hobbled across the room and let himself down with a faint grimace onto a chair by the stove. "Been over to the livery," he announced, "passing the time of day with Charlie. Quickest way I know to get a line on whatever is going on. Charlie says the town is quiet enough. He seen Bud Taylor ride in a while ago; otherwise there don't seem to be much stirring."

Croft nodded absently. He was thinking that things would liven up enough in a couple of days or so, when the roundup wagons returned and the crews came pouring into town, thirsty and with the end of a long and arduous chore to celebrate. He tossed a stack of paper into the wastebasket, got up to return the letter file to its place in the cabinet. As he turned from doing this, the door burst open and Warren Bishop strode into the office.

He looked as though he had ridden hard and long. From his ashen cheeks and the look of his blue eyes—so much like Edie's—Croft knew at once that something was very wrong. Bishop tried to speak; his lips worked but nothing came out of them. Finally, with a groan, he dug a hand into a pocket of his blanket coat and brought out a crumpled bit of paper and thrust it at Croft.

"Read that!" he cried hoarsely.

Croft recognized the writing at first glimpse, and knew a fatalistic stab of dread as he took the note from Bishop's trembling fingers. He read: *Dearest Papa. When you find this you will know that I am gone. I just couldn't leave without some word, to tell you that I am all right and you're not to worry about me. Jim and I—*"

The words seemed to blur and swim before Croft's unbelieving eyes and he gripped the paper tightly, trying to force the hurriedly penciled words to tell him more than they could. Finally he looked into the rancher's stricken face.

"When did you find this?"

"Not an hour ago," Bishop answered hollowly. "It must have been this morning sometime when that . . . that damn skunk—" His voice broke and the tears swam in his weak blue eyes, and he dashed a wrist across them.

"Pull yourself together," Croft commanded. Aware then of Homer's stammered questions he answered his deputy in a few curt words: "Edie's run off with Jim Taylor."

"Run off!" Homer echoed. "Where to?"

"The note doesn't say. Apparently Jim told her he would marry her, if she'd go with him. . . ."

"By God, he *will* marry her!" Warren Bishop cried, in a small man's weak rage. "If I have to follow them both and hold a gun on him. And if he doesn't I'll—I'll *kill* him!"

Croft moved his shoulders, trying to dislodge the leaden weight that had settled in his chest. He said gruffly, handing the paper back, "Get ahold of yourself, Warren! That sort of talk won't help any."

"Then what are you going to do about this?" Edie's father demanded.

"All I can, of course."

Homer Ingalls put in dryly, "That might not amount to much. If they've got a good start, and no hint of where they're headed for . . ."

"They took one of my horses," Bishop put in.

Croft, rubbing a fist across his moustache, was forced to admit the chances of intercepting Taylor and the girl looked small. He felt sick at heart, and also such a furious anger that he wondered just what he, himself, would do at that moment if Jim Taylor suddenly fell into his hands.

He reacted suddenly to what Bishop was saying. He made the man repeat it: "I said, I want you to come with me right now while I show this note to Bud Taylor. I saw him a minute ago, over on Main Street, but I wanted to have the law with me."

The sheriff scowled. "What good do you expect that to do? It's not likely Bud knows anything about this."

"I *mean* for him to know it! Are you going to be my witness or not?"

Ben Croft wanted no part of any of it, but after a moment's hesitation he reluctantly nodded. Like many weak men, he was afraid Warren Bishop could be capable of almost any wild thing when emotions ruled him. "All right," he said reluctantly. "I'll come. But I'm asking you to watch your step with him!"

They found Bud Taylor just locking his office door, and waited at the bottom of the steps while he checked the knob, pocketed his latchkey and came down to them—a man who moved deliberately and with a sense of his own importance in this section of Montana range. He looked them both over and pinned his attention on the sheriff as he demanded coldly,. "You got business with me?"

The lawman shook his head. "It's Bishop, here. I just came along."

Taylor switched his glance to the other rancher; Warren Bishop thrust Edie's message at him, as though not trusting himself to say anything more than, "Read this!" Bud Taylor's arrogant glance studied him a moment before he lowered his eyes to the paper.

Croft watched his eyes and his lips move as he worked his way through the note, with the manner of one to whom reading was not a favorite occupation. His head lifted, then, and handing back the paper he said, "All right. I've read it."

Color began to stain the other's cheeks. "That all you've got to say?"

"What do you expect me to say? That I approve, maybe? Well, I do like hell! This ain't exactly what I had in mind for bringing new blood into the Taylor family. That silly little blond!"

Stung, Bishop cried, "You're talking about my daughter!"

"I'm talking about my son!" the other man retorted. "He thinks he's defying me. He may learn differently before this little fling is over!"

"Bud," Ben Croft asked, "would you know where they are? Have you any notion where Jim might have taken her?"

Taylor flicked him with a glance. "If I did, I wouldn't tell *you*. It ain't any of your business!"

"It's *my* business!" Warren Bishop shouted, brandishing the paper. "He's promised my girl that he'd marry her. And I'm serving notice right now, in front of the law, that I mean to hold him to that promise. What's more, I expect you to make sure he honors it. You understand me?"

Taylor simply brushed him with a look of utter contempt and, not answering, shoved his way past Bishop and the sheriff and strode to the big gray gelding that stood at a nearby hitching post. He jerked the reins free with a movement of his wrist and flung himself into the saddle, almost without touching stirrup. Stern and erect, despite the years that put gray streaks in his hair and untrimmed brown beard, he put the spurs to his horse and rode from there without another glance at the pair who watched him go.

Warren Bishop turned to the sheriff, eyes ablaze with self-righteous anger. "You heard what I said to him! You're my witness, Croft!"

The other drew a breath. He said heavily, "Yes, Warren. I heard you put in your claim, through your daughter, for a share of Diamond T!"

"What! You think that's all I'm after? Croft, come back here!"

But the sheriff wouldn't stay to discuss it. He turned and walked away from the man, leaving him stammering in indignation. For his own part, Croft was too numbed and emptied by news of the elopement to be sure of his own emotions.

The gray horse was staggering when Bud Taylor spurred it into the Diamond T yard, never having once eased up on it during the headlong rush over the miles from town. When he threw down before the veranda of the big log-and-stone ranch house that was the heart of his widespread domain, he noticed for the first time how much he had taken out of the animal; it stood with head drooping, sweat darkening its hide and dripping into the dust. He was lucky if he hadn't ruined the horse, and he felt a pang of shame.

But he merely tossed the reins to the yard boy who came hurrying up, and with no change in the set of his features tramped up the broad steps to the veranda. Now that he was here he really didn't know why he had hurried. He had had some notion of ordering out the crew and sending them to search for his runaway son; but now that his temper had cooled a trifle he knew that had been a futile idea: Diamond T riders were scattered, some still out with the closing phases of roundup, others with the delivery herd that the foreman, Tom Andress, had started on the drive to railhead yesterday morning. The crew was no use to him in this emergency.

Roweled by angry frustration, he entered the house, crossing the big, low-ceilinged living room with its heavy, leather-slung furniture and the deep and smoke-blackened fireplace where a log was burning. He flung his weathered hat into a chair and started down the hallway leading to the room at the back of the house that served him for an office. But then a thought made him pause, and turn. On an impulse he retraced his steps and mounted the steps that led from the living room to the second story.

Ringing his spurs down the dimly lit corridor, he flung open a door and without ceremony tramped into the room where his wife sat in bed in her dressing gown, propped up against pillows, a Bible open upon her knees.

Ellen Taylor looked at him in apprehension as he dropped his big hands upon the foot of the bedframe and glared at her. She had been a pretty woman, once—pretty in the same way her son Jim was handsome—but she had never had the spirit to cope with the overpowering strength and dynamic personality of this husband of hers. In time she had retreated into semi-invalidism; the sunlight from the window fell across a face that had gone thin as it lost its youth, and hair that had been darkly lustrous now framed her face in a drab, gray tangle.

Frightened eyes peered at Bud Taylor as he pounded the foot of the bed with a fist and roared at her: "Well, that worthless son of yours has done it! He's seduced that mealy-mouthed little Bishop girl and talked her into running off with him! I suppose I could have expected some such foolishness out of him sooner or later; but what I want to know is, where'd he get the money?

"He never got it from me—*that's* certain!" The rancher went on, his voice rising as his anger mounted, oblivious to the shock and grief his news had put in the woman's face. "I've always seen to it he was kept on a tight rein, because I knew he had no sense about anything. But even he wouldn't have had the guts to try a thing like this without having a pocketful, or knowing where he could get it. . . ." His piercing stare settled on the woman in the bed. "It wouldn't be that *you* could tell me something about this?"

Her hands trembled where they lay upon the Bible, but her voice was steady enough: "You know I don't have a cent I could have given him!"

He acknowledged the fact with a grunt. "Just as well! You'd have given it to him, all right, if he asked for it. All his life you done your best to spoil that kid and turn him into something just as weak as yourself. Something a hell of a lot less than I wanted in a son!"

"Tell me, Howard," she said quietly, "would *anyone* ever have had a chance of becoming what you wanted in a son?"

Confronted by the question, he made an impatient slicing gesture with a rope-scarred palm; but then he paused at his own thought. "Maybe just one," he said slowly, "come to think of it: that young fellow, Croft. He's so damn stubborn he drives me crazy, but at least he's a man. Yeah, I think I could have done something with a boy like him."

"Could you really? I wonder if he would have let you. . . ."

Something in her words left him staring, bemused and puzzled without quite knowing why. But then he dismissed the sheriff from his thoughts, once more reverting to the problem of his son.

"That damned idiot!" Bud Taylor fumed. "Worst of it is, he's making a fool not only of himself, but of *me!* If there was only some way of finding out where he thinks he's going, so he could be headed off!"

"You're thinking I might know," his wife said. "Well, I don't!"

"I'm not so sure," her husband retorted, studying her ravaged face. "I know damn well he's always told you things I could never have pried out of him with a crowbar. I also know damn well he hated this ranch, and this country. . . .

You're certain he never let drop so much as a hint as to where he'd rather be if he had his chance to leave it?"

When she didn't at once answer, Taylor read the truth in her eyes. "Ha! I hit paydirt that time, didn't I?" And, striding around the side of the bed, he leaned and placed a heavy hand upon her frail shoulder. "Answer my question!"

She winced and tried to draw away; her eyes wavered and fell and her head drooped as she said at last, in a low voice, "He—he sometimes talked of San Francisco. But that doesn't mean—"

"Frisco!" Taylor straightened, a light kindling in his eyes. "By God, I think you've hit it! That does sound like the way he'd think!" He fell to pacing, bootheels squealing on the fine hardwood floor; he whirled suddenly, and a pointing finger stabbed the air. "Damn it, yes! That's it! And it means he'd have to go to Flynn's Creek to take the westbound. With that piece of fluff on his hands he can't travel fast. If I ride all night, I ought to catch up with him there before he has a chance to board the train!"

"And if you do?" Ellen Taylor ventured to ask; her voice frightened. "Howard, don't be too hard on him. Please! Remember, he's your son!"

But her husband was already gone, hurrying away down the corridor, with purpose in the sound of his reaching stride. She dropped the hand she had lifted; her face, as she settled back against the pillows with eyes closed and lips working, held the look of one who knows a fatalistic sense of coming disaster.

CHAPTER XII

IN HIS OWN ROOM, Bud Taylor prepared for what he knew was going to be a long and probably chilly night in the saddle, changing into worn but serviceable trail garb and a sheep-lined canvas coat that was spotted with grease and impregnated with the smells of horse sweat and tobacco, but felt as natural as his own skin. At the last moment, obeying some vague impulse that was probably born of his dark mood, he buckled on his belt and walnut-handled six-shooter, afterward pulling on a battered Stetson and tramping downstairs to the kitchen.

It was too early for supper to be ready and he impatiently refused the ranch cook's offer to fix him something. Instead he drained off a cup of coffee, standing up while the man put together a couple of meat sandwiches and wrapped them; Taylor slipped them into a pocket of his coat. At the corral he roped out a big, solid black animal with sound wind and staying qualities, and put his gear on it. With the sun dragging low over the timbered hills on the western horizon, he lifted into the saddle and pointed his horse south in the direction of the railroad.

With a long haul ahead of him, he used the black more reasonably than he had the other mount he'd punished on his blind chase from town. He kept to a steady gait: a running walk that the horse could keep up tirelessly, eating away the miles as the short autumn day drew out in a final golden wash of slanting light and stretching shadow. The low-lying clouds over the hills fired up with glowing reds that faded into gray ashes, and dusk came upon the Montana rangeland.

Somewhere ahead, probably after midnight, he figured, he would come upon the camp where Tom Andress and the trail crew would be bedded down with the delivery herd that had started yesterday on its way to the shipping pens at Flynn's Creek. Bud Taylor had included this in his calculations: there he could get a fresh mount, hot grub, perhaps even an hour or two of rest if he thought it might safely be spared. Then he would push on again, to reach Flynn's Creek before ten in the morning when the west-bound was due.

He never doubted for a moment, that that was where he would find his son. He thought no further, knowing only that Jim Taylor was in for a very bad time. This latest stupidity was something the young no-good was not going to be allowed to forget in a hurry. . . .

Breaking out the sandwiches, he ate them in the saddle, dry, without pausing. Dusk settled and became night; a chill wind flowed down across the darkening earth, pressing against his back and right side, making him pull up the coat and fasten it. Bud Taylor rode deep in the saddle, his shoulders feeling only the first hint of ache that would be a burning torture before this night was finished. A sky that was heavy and encrusted with a glittering of stars, immense as only a Montana sky can be, pressed down upon him; the steady slog of his horse's hooves, with the accompanying rhythm of creaking saddle gear and the rush of the night wind in his ears, made up the night's music. There was no moon.

He had only a dim notion of the time when he first caught sight of a spot of fire, glowing on the plain ahead of him and a little off the direct trail. In such blackness, even a campfire could be visible for miles. Taylor watched it, frowning, as the black carried him steadily nearer. It could hardly be Andress' camp; he should not be coming upon that for long hours yet. If this was the Diamond T trail herd, then it was sadly behind schedule.

But there was another possibility. Bad accidents some-times happened when you were handling a bunch of cattle:

a rider's horse could fall with him, or he could be thrown and gored or trampled. Since the crew had no wagon for this short drive, subsisting on saddle rations alone, there was no way Tom Andress could carry a hurt man with him. He'd have had to make him comfortable and leave him by the trail. If by any chance at all this was the camp of one of his own injured crewmen, Bud Taylor wanted to know.

He pulled aside and rode in on it. The fire had been built in a little bay of rocks and trees and the dancing light of the flames showed him the signs of a fair-sized camp. Blanket rolls and gear lay about, and he could hear horses stirring and feeding; but he could see nothing at all of the men. This made him uneasy, but definitely curious. Just at the edge of the light he pulled up and a hand brushed aside his coat and rested on the butt of the gun in his holster. He called sharply, "Is anyone here? Speak up!"

To his right a voice said, "Mister, we're a little careful about strangers that come riding in on our fire!"

Bud Taylor's head whipped around. He saw the dim shape of the man who had stepped out of the tree shadows, and the gleam of the rifle he held across his front at high point. Gauging the rifle, Taylor frowned and took his own hand away from holster, placing it on his saddlehorn instead. He said, "I was riding by. Thought it might be somebody I knew, camped here."

"It might, at that." A second man stepped into the fire-light. Taylor looked at him, and his body stiffened as he recognized the blandly sinister face of Link Fannin.

"You!" he exclaimed.

Now they seemed to fade into sight from every direction; he counted four from the corners of his eyes, while he kept his stare pinned on the rustler chief. "What are the lot of you doing here?"

Fannin stood hipshot, completely at his ease. "It's a big country, and a free one. We got a right."

The one who had first challenged Taylor was a gaunt,

red-headed man named, he thought, Agard or something similar. Still hostile, he said now, "What's *he* doing riding through on the trail to Flynn's Creek? You don't suppose he could have got wind of—"

His chief cut him short. "The man's got a herd camped somewhere up ahead. Reason enough for him to be here."

But something in that exchange started an alarming suspicion in Bud Taylor. "It wouldn't be," he demanded with forthright bluntness, "you got ideas about that shipping herd? By God, if I thought so . . ."

One of the men laughed scornfully. "Listen to him talk up to us! Sounds real tough, don't he?"

"Well, he *is* tough," Link Fannin replied with indulgent good humor.

"Some day," a new voice said tightly, "he's going to try to put all that weight on the wrong man, at the wrong time. . . ."

Bud Taylor saw him then: the gambler, Gil Ivy, his plug hat and white shirt and fancy waistcoat looking out of place in this company of rough-clad riders. Ivy met his stare, seeming to sense the rancher's cold astonishment. "You look surprised."

"I thought you'd left the country!"

"Just because you told me to? Don't forget, I'm still owed two thousand dollars. I don't go without it!"

"I've already told you you'll never get a dime from me!"

The gambler wagged his head. "And I believe you," he agreed. His voice changed then, filled with all the hatred he felt for this man. "So I figured out another way to get it. You're going to wish you'd settled for the two thousand!"

Link Fannin must have thought the man was saying too much. He started to say so, but Gil Ivy waved him off. "Don't worry—he's not going to repeat a word of this. He's not going to get the chance!" His right hand moved into the open, holding the ugly derringer that he carried in his clothing; seeing it, Bud Taylor for the first time knew he was really in deadly peril. He gave a start and his own hand dropped but stopped short of the opening of his coat, coming to rest on his slabby thigh as the derringer's black muzzle settled on him.

Ivy said, in harsh triumph, "This is better payment than I could have asked for throwing me down the office stairs! I never figured on having the chance to tell him exactly what's going to happen to that shipping herd, and to his spoiled brat of a son!"

The breath caught in Taylor's throat. "Have you got my boy here?" he cried hoarsely.

"Oh, no. He should be well on his way to Flynn's Creek by now, to wait for us and for the herd. We let him believe all he has to do is intercept the payment for it, and we'll let him keep half. Well, he always was a damn fool. He'd have to be, to think he's going to get anything out of us besides a bullet. . . ."

With a shout of fury, Bud Taylor pawed at his holster. As the gun slid free he saw the muzzle flare of the gambler's derringer, almost thought he felt the concussion of the bullet passing within inches of his ear. Then he had his own weapon leveled and fired, and saw Gil Ivy driven backward by the thrust of the bullet.

There were yells from Fannin's men as more than one of them went for a gun. Taylor was concentrating on his horse, trying to rein him about and at the same time kick the spurs home and send him away from there. The black, terrified by gunfire, lost its head and simply backed in a tight circle, dust and hot ashes from the fire stirring in a cloud under its trampling hooves. Swearing insanely, Taylor pulled it out of that and as he did so heard the roar of a gun and felt something strike a heavy blow in the middle of his body. He dropped his own weapon, grabbed at the horn to keep from being swept from the saddle.

Confused, numbed by pain, blinded by fireglow and muzzleblast, he knew enough to hang on to reins and saddlehorn and kick the black with both spurred heels. The animal squealed and leaped frantically; the jar of all four hooves striking earth together nearly shook him from his place. Guns seemed to be hammering from all sides. He knew he had been hit a second time. Then somehow the black got itself lined out and was off at a run, and the guns and yells faded and he knew he was leaving the campfire behind him.

They would be after him, though, as soon as they got into their own saddles; Bud Taylor didn't doubt that for an instant. With what he could still command of his senses, as every pound of the black's hooves jarred pain through him, he knew that he was a dead man if he failed somehow to elude them.

He began to doubt he had the strength to stick it out.

Unmeasured time passed. Suddenly he felt as though he had come back from a great distance, to find that motion and sound had ceased. He was still in the saddle, bent over the neck of his horse, but the animal was no longer moving. Forcing his head up, he peered about him. There was the bright mesh of the stars overhead, putting down a faint light. He saw dimly the shapes of trees, and of boulders fallen from a rim that lifted at his right hand. Bud Taylor listened for sounds of his pursuers, but heard nothing except the night wind sweeping across sere autumn grassland and swaying the pinetree branches.

Gathering his strength and focusing his dazed thoughts, he spoke to the black and sent it angling up the slope until crowding tree trunks halted it. Here he was in an angle formed by two of the fallen boulders nearly the size of small houses; it was the best he could do.

He reached an exploring hand in under his coat, felt the warm wetness that told him he was badly wounded. Clinging to the saddle, fighting weakness and pain, he listened for a distant shout or any other sound that would tell him his enemies were still hunting. If there was any luck left in him, they might miss him here. After that, it was up to the black.

No hope of going on now, or trying to elude Fannin's men and reach the Diamond T camp. He would have to turn back. The horse knew its home corral; it would take him there if he could only manage, somehow, through blind determination and a horseman's instinct, to stay in the saddle.

The last of Fannin's riders came straggling back to the campfire at last; swinging down, he met Fannin's questioning look with a shake of the head. "Not a sign of him. Hell! Who could find anything on a night as dark as this one?"

Link Fannin, for once, wasn't showing any trace of amusement. He stood and stared at nothing, the fireglow making pinpoints of brightness in his narrowed eyes. Cash Agard said gruffly, "He won't get far. I tell you, I know when I hit something, and I tagged the bastard good!"

They waited, then, and after a long moment their chief moved his shoulders and said, "All right, let him go. No matter. It's too late now for anybody to stop us. But we'll move on all the same, just in case someone might have been in earshot, and get curious about the guns." He looked down at the body of Gil Ivy, sprawled at his feet where Bud Taylor's hasty bullet had dumped him; Link Fannin nudged the gambler with his boottoe, and the dead man gave limply.

"One less split," he grunted, and dismissed the killing as simply as that. "A couple of you take him and dump him in the rocks somewhere. The rest get packed and let's move out of here!"

CHAPTER XIII

THE SAME MAN who came into town to get the doctor also dropped around at Sheriff Croft's shack and woke him up to tell him the news. What he could tell was little enough.

He was the ranch cook, an ex-cowboy with a crippled leg. He knew only that Bud Taylor's horse had brought him home a couple of hours past midnight, Taylor clinging to the saddle and badly wounded in two places. Ben Croft hurriedly dressed and prepared to ride out to Diamond T.

When he got there, Sam Elgin had already been working on the hurt man and done as much as he could to make him comfortable; the doctor met Croft in the hallway outside Taylor's bedroom, and nodded with approval. "Glad you made it," he said. "Bud's asking for you. He's some anxious."

"How is he?" Croft wanted to know.

"Reasonable good shape, considering the blood he's lost. He took one bullet under the ribs; that came near gutting him. Another one lodged in his shoulder and I had to dig it out. A lesser man would never have managed to hang to the saddle that long!" The doctor added, "You better get in there and talk to him; maybe that'll quiet him down and he can start mending."

Croft nodded and walked into the bedroom.

Bud Taylor looked a size or two smaller than life, lying there on the bed swathed in bandages. A turned-down lamp burning on a table made his face look waxen, almost as colorless as the pillow. His wife sat near him in a cane rocker, a forlorn figure with a robe clutched about her and one of her husband's hands in hers. He seemed to cling to it as though to life itself.

Ben Croft had never thought he would feel anything but dislike toward this arrogant man, but listening to his harsh breathing he couldn't help a pang of pity for someone so strong, who had been laid flat by a couple of insignificant scraps of metal.

The rancher's eyes opened; they appeared glazed by pain. They rested on Ben Croft's face for a moment as though not recognizing him. Then a fire blazed in them and Taylor tried to lift his head from the pillow. He let it drop back with a gasp; speech came from him, a hoarse whisper that strengthened as he forced out the words: "Croft? So

100

you're here, are you? Well, you sure weren't around when I could have used you, this evening. They tried to kill me, damn them!"

Ben Croft ignored the gratuitously slighting remark; he had learned by now that this man couldn't open his mouth without some such thing emerging. Perhaps it was a necessary way of bolstering his sense of his own worth. The sheriff said merely, "Who was it, Bud? Who shot you?"

"One of Link Fannin's crowd. And that tinhorn . . . that Gil Ivy. I got *him*, anyway. Plugged him solid!"

"If you have the strength to tell me what happened," Croft said, "I'd like to hear it. . . ."

"You're damn well going to hear it!" the rancher snorted, and though it cost him a visible effort he poured it out; he was gasping before he finished, and the big, rope-tough hand lying upon the blanket that covered him trembled with fatigue. "It's up to you, Croft!" he finished in a voice that shook. "There ain't anybody else! You got to stop those conniving crooks . . . and save that fool kid of mine from his own stupidity! You hear me?"

"I hear you," the sheriff said coldly. "I think I know my job. The trouble is, I just don't know if there's time."

"Listen to me!" the hurt man cried, and he actually struggled up onto an elbow though his wife cried out and tried to hold him back. "I never asked any man for favors; and God knows, I guess, you don't owe me or my family none. But I'm asking you to do this. And I'm sayin' please!"

Ben Croft looked at him a long moment; slowly, he nodded. "I'll do what I can," he said. "I can't promise anything more."

But that seemed to satisfy Bud Taylor; he grunted and dropped back, panting. Sam Elgin had reentered the room after washing up, and he heard the last part of this. He sternly told the hurt man, "Be more careful with yourself, Taylor, or I won't guarantee the outcome!"

The rancher waved him aside with a trembling hand, muttering testily, "All right, all right!" He had thought of something more and he demanded hoarsely, "Somebody fetch paper and a pen. Ought to be on the table yonder." Elgin located, amid its litter, a pad of foolscap, and took a reservoir pen from his own coat pocket. "Try to write plainer than you do filling out them prescriptions of yours, Doc," Bud Taylor admonished him gruffly. "Make me out a power of attorney, naming Croft here my sole agent with authority to collect payment for that herd at Flynn's Creek. Make it sound legal if you can."

Elgin cocked an eyebrow at Croft in a look of surprise, but he did as he was asked; for a moment the scratch of the pen over the pad of cheap paper was the only sound in the night stillness. Finished, he read aloud what he had written. "That all right?"

"Fine, fine!" the hurt man said impatiently. "Give it here and let me sign it." His wife held up the pad for him and he scrawled his signature, adding, "This ought to spike Fannin's guns for him. And it'll show that damned fool youngster of mine where to head in! Take it with you, Croft. Use it if you need it."

Sober of face, Croft folded the crude document and put it away in his pocket. "If I need it," he agreed. "Right now I got to get started. If I take the trail and keep pushing, with luck I should hit Flynn's Creek by sometime tomorrow afternoon. Still a chance of making it before the herd can have been moved onto the cars . . . and before any money changes hands."

Sam Elgin protested: "You go up against Link Fannin, you'll need help! You know that, don't you?"

Croft looked at him, appreciating his concern. But he said, "There'll be Tom Andress and the drive crew, remember. I imagine that if I send up the distress signal I can count on them to pitch in." Impatiently he turned toward the door, ridden hard by the necessity that lay upon him. But there he halted a moment, hearing the man in the bed say his name.

"Good luck, Croft," the rancher muttered. "And don't let 'em hurt my boy . . . even if he ain't too damn much good!"

It was the nearest to sentiment Ben Croft had ever

seen in the tough old man, and it surprised him into silence for a moment. Then he nodded and said, "I'll do my best." He saw Ellen Taylor's lips move silently and wondered if she was praying. He turned on his heel and strode out of the room.

Flynn's Creek was an ugly town, with hardly a tree to break the angular barrenness of its criss-cross of streets and blocky frame buildings. But it had the railhead, and so it prospered. Saddle-galled and bone-weary, Ben Croft picked up the dazzle of sunlight on steel as he came down the last slope on a horse that stumbled under him, played out from the unrelenting pace he'd been forced to keep it to.

He saw, also, the ballooning saffron dust above the loading pens that sprawled near the tracks just where they crossed the creek on a wooden trestle. He heard the bawling of cattle and the fainter voices of yelling men who pushed them into the cars, and his spirit took a lift, dispelling some of the aching tiredness.

If that was the Diamond T herd, still loading, then it looked as though he had made it in time.

He urged the horse the remaining distance, coming in on the town past the pens and the siding where a work engine, idling near the chutes, puffed smoke from its stack. Before he was near enough to read brands, he saw a couple of faces he recognized and gave a sigh of relief. He reined in as a Diamond T hand named Gifford leaped down from a fence, wiping sweat from his face on his neckcloth. Ben Croft said, "Looks like you've about finished the job here."

The men looked at him in surprise. "Why, howdy, Sheriff. Had no idea you were in town." He got a better look at the other's dusty, unshaven appearance, and the worn-out horse. His eyes narrowed. "You been ridin'! Maybe you had reason to think you better be here. . . ."

Croft caught him up on that quickly. "Why? Is something wrong?"

"Maybe, maybe not. But Link Fannin and I don't know

how many of his boys are around, and they been keeping an eye on this operation ever since we started loading. I can't imagine why; but I know I don't like it. Makes a man nervous!"

The sheriff considered this. He asked, "Where's Tom?"

Gifford jerked his head toward the main buildings of the town. "He went up to the hotel a few minutes ago, to look up Ed Denton and collect for the herd."

"He went alone?"

The man nodded; then something he appeared to read in the sheriff's face narrowed his eyes. "You think there might be trouble with Fannin? Let me call the boys together and we'll give you a hand."

Croft was tempted, knowing he could use any help he could get; but he shook his head. He had to know about Tom Andress. If Tom had fallen into the outlaw's hands, at the first show of a fight by the Diamond T men his life could be forfeit. The sheriff said, "Thanks, but for the time being I can handle this alone. You might keep your ears open, though; could be I'll need you in a hurry!"

"Whatever you say," the puncher told him; but he was fully alarmed now. Croft could feel his stare following as he turned his fagged horse and pointed him toward the heart of town.

His own fatigue bothered him. He had been in the saddle since the small hours of the night before, with hardly a break in all that time, and though he was keyed up with the tension of what lay ahead he was not sure of his reflexes. At a water trough on the shady side of the street he pulled in and dismounted, to sink his hands to the wrists and then splash cold water from the spout over his dust-rimed and stubble-bearded face. That helped get through the lethargy that clung to him. While his horse drank he stretched to ease the burning ache out of his shoulders, and then, as he stood looking upstreet and gauging the temper of the town, loosened his gun in the holster and let it slide back again.

Someone spoke his name. He jerked about, to discover Edie Bishop standing beneath the wooden awning that roofed the sidewalk, where he had failed to see her in the shadows. He flipped his bronc's reins about the tooth-scarred pole of a hitchrack, and stepped up to join her.

"Edie!" he exclaimed. "Are you all right?"

She nodded, but her face held an unnatural pallor and the hand that seized his sleeve was trembling. "Oh, Ben!" she cried in a voice she seemed hardly able to control. "Thank God! I'm so frightened!"

She was pathetic in her evident terror, but Croft couldn't resist a small, sour dig. "Frightened? But you've got Jim to look out for you. . . ."

A shudder went through her. "Ben, he's changed! Just in the last day . . . the last few hours. He won't talk to me. He's been drinking. He, and those men that he met here—"

"Link Fannin's men?"

Either the name meant nothing to her, or she was too distraught to make the connection. "I'm afraid of them! And when I finally insisted on Jim's telling me what business he had with them, he—he *hit* me!"

She turned her head slightly and he could see, now, the slight swelling and discoloration of her cheek. When she spoke again she had to struggle with the convulsive sobs that broke her speech. "So I just . . . walked out of the hotel. I don't think he even noticed. I was going down to the stable to get my horse, and ride home. Alone, if I had to! But now, you're here—you'll help. Ben, please be good to me. I . . . I'm so alone, and scared!"

"You'll be all right," he said, less gently than he might have under the circumstances. He thought he could have actually taken her into his arms, as they stood close together there under the arcade, but he made no move to touch her. Instead he asked, "Do you know anything about Tom Andress?"

She shook her head, impatient with the question. "I haven't seen him. We did pass a trail crew, and Jim told me he was with it; but we swung wide around them and didn't stop." Her fingers dug into his arm. "Oh, Ben, take me home. Please!"

Looking at her, he wondered suddenly what had ever made him think he was in love with her. Beneath a certain youthful prettiness she was, he knew now, shallow and self-centered. She didn't really care if Jim Taylor might be in trouble. She hadn't cared yesterday how her father would feel to learn she had run away. Croft found himself thinking bleakly that if she knew she was partly responsible for Bud Taylor's getting shot and nearly killed, it probably wouldn't touch her at all. She'd never given a thought to anyone but herself—and she was not mature enough to start now. . . .

He took a slow breath, rubbed a hand across his moustache and the stubble on his unshaven jaw. "All right, Edie," he told her. "Try to get ahold of yourself. You'll be taken care of. Just now, there's something else I've got to—"

He broke off, his head lifting sharply.

Perhaps half a block ahead, a clot of men had suddenly made their appearance, coming down the broad steps of the hotel whose bulk dominated this side of the dusty street. He knew at once who they were, recognized Cash Agard by his rusty mop of hair and the beanpole figure that even a bulky sheepskin coat could not disguise. One of the others would be Link Fannin, he was sure. They halted and stood motionless, staring in his direction.

His face grim, Ben Croft looked quickly about. Just beside him was the entrance to a milliner's shop, the show window holding a display of frilly bonnets in the latest extravagant style. Quickly he took Edie Bishop's elbow and turned her toward the doorway, saying sharply, "Get in there quick! And stay out of sight. There's going to be trouble!"

"Ben!" Her voice quavered with fear. As he opened the door for her she clutched at him, crying, "Don't leave me alone! Please!" He didn't have much patience. He removed her fingers from his arm and closed the door, her frantic appeal still sounding in his ears as he turned and looked back up the street to see what Fannin's men were doing.

They had spread out a little, still watching him. One moved around a tie rail and circled out into the street, and Croft got a look at his face and recognized him: it was the Diamond T hand, Mort Keel. That jarred a grunt of surprise from him, and he said under his breath, "So you're in this, too!" Well, wherever you found Jim Taylor, his special crony was pretty certain to be around.

A chill autumn wind raked the street, lifting a stinging curtain of dust and tumbling loose papers before it and plucking at hatbrims and coattails. Ben Croft ducked his head and slitted his eyes until it passed. And then, waiting no longer on his enemies, he started walking straight toward them until he had reached the corner of the shop; there, without warning, a quick sidestep took him into the alleyway, and an adjoining building cut him off from all view of them.

They hadn't expected that; there was a quick shout of alarm, carrying thinly above the noise that drifted from the loading pens. Croft slid the gun from his holster and he turned and went at a run between the buildings, heading away from the street.

He knew the outlaws would stop him if they could. And he had a feeling time was running out.

CHAPTER XIV

HOVERING near the archway separating the hotel lobby from the adjoining bar, his nerves tight-strung despite the liquor he had consumed to loosen them, Jim Taylor had waited nervously as he watched the half dozen men lined up at the bar over their drinks. Finally, as though aware of him for the first time, Link Fannin caught his eye in the bar mirror. The rustler looked at him coolly, gave him a curt nod that heightened his tensions and caused the breath to catch shallowly in his throat.

A moment later, with studied casualness, the men at the bar finished their business there. Empty glasses were set aside. Spurs chimed as the lot of them went trailing in a noisy group toward the street entrance. The closing of the glassed double doors shut away the sound of them.

Now it was up to Jim Taylor.

In the mirror, again, he looked at the one remaining customer, seated at a table with a bowler hat beside him and a carpetbag on the floor by his chair, as he worked at a bowl of chili and crackers. The barman was putting away his bottles and clearing off the empty glasses left by Fannin's men. On the lobby wall, at Jim's back, a pendulum clock bonged a couple of times, striking the hour. He straightened his shoulders, settled his breathing, and with determination pushed open the batwings.

Ed Denton was a small and wiry businessman of forty, going bald, and with a perpetual nervous scowl. He looked up from his food as the newcomer approached the table. "Why, hello! It's young Taylor, isn't it?" The cattle dealer stood, shook hands, and seated himself again, while Jim pulled back a chair and eased into it.

"I'll have to admit I'm glad to see somebody I know," Denton said. "I didn't much like the looks of that crowd that just walked out of here. Did you happen to notice them?" Jim Taylor hastily shook his head, murmuring a denial. "Thought you might know them," the other said, still showing his uneasiness as he reached for his coffee cup. "A bunch of cutthroats, in *my* book!" Abruptly he changed the subject. "How's your pa?"

"Fine, fine," the younger man mumbled. He drew a breath, remembering his job. "I guess that herd should just about be on the cars by now. So if you're ready, I suppose we may as well settle up."

Denton peered at him, puzzled. "I understood I was doing business with Tom Andress. . . ."

Jim tried to sound offhand and convincing. "I'm taking over for Tom. Happened to be in town on another matter, so Pa thought I might handle this, too." Now came the most ticklish matter of all. His throat suddenly dry, he added, "I hope you're prepared to deal in cash?"

Ed Denton made a face, but he nodded. "Yes, I'm well aware your pa's old-fashioned about dealing in hard money instead of bank paper—even though it can be a damned inconvenience." He pushed back his empty dishes, and leaned to pick up the carpetbag and place it on the table.

"It's right here," he said; and Jim Taylor let the breath ease from his throat, this hurdle being safely passed. "Soon as my man comes up from the loading pen with the final tally, I'm frankly going to be glad to turn this over to you. Those toughs that were in here a moment ago: I couldn't help wondering what might have happened if they'd known I had better than thirty thousand dollars in this bag!"

Jim Taylor didn't answer.

Pulling a heavy gold watch from his pocket, Denton checked the time and stuffed it back again. "How about a drink while we're waiting?" he suggested; and Jim Taylor, realizing he could use another one, quickly agreed. The cattle buyer signaled and the bartender brought bottle and glasses. Denton poured for them both. Young Taylor nervously seized his glass and drained it off; but the other was more deliberate, swishing each sip of the whiskey around inside his mouth before he swallowed it.

And then, outside in the street, men were yelling suddenly, and boardwalk planks rattled under the pound of running boots. Denton's head jerked around toward the door and he exclaimed, "What do you suppose is going on out there?" Jim Taylor didn't answer, but a premonition lifted him to his feet and took him to the street entrance for a look through the glass.

At once he saw Fannin and Keel and the others; from the way they were acting he knew something must have

109

gone very wrong. A coldness began to creep along his nerves as he listened, to make out what they were shouting:

"*There he goes!*"

"*Stop him, damn it!*"

The bartender, watching Taylor, demanded, "What do you see?"

He shook his head. "Nothing much." And that was true enough when he said it, for the outlaws had suddenly passed out of his line of sight, moving off downstreet as though in pursuit of something. He started to put a hand on the doorknob, then instead pulled it back and rubbed both palms along his pantlegs to dry them of a sudden clammy moisture.

Whatever was happening, he had his own responsibility: Ed Denton and that carpetbag with thirty-odd thousand dollars in cash. He turned and walked back to the table. "Bunch of drunks, probably." He tried to sound indifferent and unconcerned as he forced himself to resume his seat, though he felt that every nerve was strung tight as a wire ready to jerk him to his feet again. Denton said something, but he only half heard what it was and grunted unintelligibly.

The cattle buyer hauled out his watch again, looked at it and snapped the case shut with an irritable gesture. "I'm thinking I better get down to the pens," he said, "and find out how much longer they're going to be. . . ."

"*Don't!*" Jim Taylor exclaimed sharply; and then as the other's puzzled stare pinned him, added lamely, "I mean, they're bound to be finished pretty soon. Let me pay for a round, while we're waiting." But he could sense a question forming in Denton's frown, as though the man was beginning to find something very strange here. He tried to keep his hand from shaking as he leaned to pick up the bottle.

He froze, his head turning at the creak of a floorboard just beyond the rear hallway entrance, a few feet away. He stared at the man who stood motionless in the opening.

Ben Croft returned his look, still working to control his breathing while he listened for any sound to warn him his enemies had pursued him in his flight across lots and along the alleyway, clear to the back entrance to the hotel. For the moment he seemed to have eluded them; he left his gun in his holster, but kept his hand on the butt, as he emerged into the barroom. Jim Taylor, the bartender, the stranger with the carpetbag on the table in front of him— they all watched him as he approached. He looked at the stranger and asked bluntly, "Your name Denton?"

The man nodded. His eyes dropped from the newcomer's beard-shagged cheeks, to the badge he revealed on pushing open the front of his windbreaker.

"Mine's Croft—sheriff of this county. I've got something here for you to look at, Mr. Denton."

He dug it from his shirt pocket; the cattle buyer's frown deepened as he unfolded the paper and read what it contained. Handing the paper back he said, "I know Bud Taylor's signature. But just what is this supposed to mean, Sheriff?"

"It means what it says: it's a power of attorney, authorizing me to collect from you for delivery of that shipping herd down at the pens." A glance at Jim Taylor showed him the stunned look that slackened the young fellow's jaw. "You like to see it, Jim?"

When Jim reached for the paper Croft shook his head, jerking it back from his fingers. Holding it for him, he watched the other's eyes track back and forth along the lines of writing. Afterward young Taylor tried a couple of times before he managed words. "I—I don't understand!"

Croft lacked the time or patience to beat around the bush with him. Returning the paper to his pocket he said, "Maybe you'll understand this: your pa knows what you've got yourself mixed up in. Last night, trying to get here and head you off, he ran into trouble and Gil Ivy nearly did for him. So he asked me to come in his place."

Jim Taylor had turned white. "Pa's hurt?"

"He's bad hurt. He thinks he dropped Ivy for good, but he took a couple of bullets doing it. Luckily his horse brought him home, and Doc Elgin did good work on him. Even

111

then, his main concern was trying to save you from something that was too much for you to cope with. That's why he signed this thing and asked me to ride over with it." His voice roughened. "Maybe you think I'm lying to you?"

But there was suddenly no argument left in the other man. He shook his head, making a limp gesture. He said dully, "I wondered why Ivy never showed up this morning with the rest. When I asked, Fannin put me off. . . ."

Ed Denton found his voice then. "Sheriff, are you suggesting it's Link Fannin and his outfit I've been seeing around town this morning? My God! No wonder I didn't like the looks of them!" His face shone with sweat suddenly. "You've got to *do* something! I'm carrying thirty thousand in cash. . . ." His hands clutched the carpetbag.

Ben Croft nodded. "I know that," he said. "It's the reason I'm here." In the same instant, boots struck the veranda; the street door was wrenched suddenly open, and Mort Keel halted with gun in hand and a boot lifted across the threshold.

Keel saw the sheriff. At once, a startled yell broke from him, directed at those in the street: "Hey! He's here! Damn it, I said he'd got past you!" And then his gun barrel dropped level and threw a hasty bullet down the length of the room.

The thunderous explosion sent the bartender to the duck boards behind his mahogany barricade, almost before the bullet slammed into the wall behind Croft; Denton likewise lost hardly any more time in dropping to the floor. The sheriff, half crouching, got his own weapon dug out of the holster and fired back, the long barrel almost resting on the carpetbag set on the table in front of him. But Mort Keel had ducked back through the door opening by that time, and Croft's bullet drilled empty space.

He could hear the man shouting again, calling for reinforcements: "Hurry, damn it! Do I have to take him by myself? You want that money, or don't you?"

Keel's shadow fell darkly across the frosted glass of the one closed wing of the double doors. Mouth grim, Ben

Croft switched his aim and punched two shots at the shadow.

The glass went with a smash and a shower of splinters. Mort Keel screamed once and Croft had a glance, through the broken window, as the renegade Diamond T puncher staggered and dropped to the floor of the porch, obviously hit.

At once Croft was hurrying forward, smoking gun ready. The bartender, rising into sight behind his counter, cried out, "For Christ sake, don't turn my place of business into a battleground!" Croft hardly gave him more than an irritated glance; he didn't see what he could be expected to do about this. He reached the open door, glimpsing Keel sprawled just beyond. In trying to discover how badly the puncher was hurt, he had to show himself for a moment; the limp shape of the man lay on its back with mouth open and eyes staring, and a mass of blood where the bullet had struck Keel high in the chest.

Then, out in the street, somebody let go with a rifle.

Croft never even saw who it was. The waspish report slapped echoes against the lifts of false-fronted buildings, and Ben Croft felt the shocking impact of something that struck his left shoulder and sent him reeling backward. He caught himself at the edge of the door to steady himself; he felt no pain, but looking down saw the rip in the material of his canvas coat. Switching hands briefly on the revolver, he checked and his exploring fingers found the first warm leaking of blood.

As he hugged the wall beside the door a wave of nausea hit him, and quickly passed. Just what was Link Fannin willing to pay, he wondered, for that carpetbag and its contents? He looked at the bartender's white face and demanded irritably, "You got a gun of some kind back there?"

"No!" The denial was too emphatic. Why didn't he just say he was having no part in this fight? Of the two others in the room, Croft had already seen that Jim Taylor had no gun and he doubted very much if Ed Denton did. It looked as though this was entirely up to him.

Upstairs, doors banged and voices of the hotel's guests called frightened questions. Ben Croft's shoulder wound was already starting to thaw and he set his teeth against the fire that was gnawing at it. Though he listened for further action in the street, for the moment he heard nothing; yet he didn't dare leave his post by the door, for it was imperative that he keep the veranda cleared. A second door led in through the hotel lobby. If he wasn't alert he could have them coming at him from both directions at once. . . .

Then something made him think of still another danger, something the pain in his shoulder must have jarred from his mind. He started to turn, remembering that back hallway through which he himself had entered the barroom, but he was just too late. For even as he moved, he heard the voice that spoke from there.

He could never have missed the false heartiness, the cold-blooded amusement that edged Link Fannin's mocking smile. "Now, Sheriff! You just stay the way you are. I ain't forgetting I owe you for one of my boys, that one you killed over by Squaw Head last month. It wouldn't be hard to put a bullet in you. . . ."

CHAPTER XV

BEN CROFT went very still. From the corners of his eyes, without moving his head, he could see into the mirror behind the bar. There was the bartender, motionless, back to back with his own reflection; and yonder, the table with the bag of money sitting on top of it, and Denton and Jim Taylor on their feet and frozen in ludicrous positions as they stared toward the hall doorway. The mirror's frame cut off any view of Link Fannin himself.

But now bootleather scuffed on floorboards and Fannin's reflection swam into his line of sight. It was odd indeed to see him like that, in profile, his eyes and the faintly gleaming barrel of his gun apparently pointing off somewhere in another direction, so that Croft had to remind himself they were really trained directly at him, just waiting for him to make a foolish move. Ben Croft held the breath shallowly in his throat, aware that he had never been so close to death.

"Let's get rid of that gun, Sheriff," the outlaw said pleasantly. "Let's just pitch it out through the door, onto the porch. Then we won't be tempted, will we?"

Croft hesitated, but he really had no choice. Stolidly, his face a mask, he gave the weapon a toss and watched it slide to a stop out there on the splintered boards of the veranda, not far from Mort Keel's motionless bootheel. To have resisted would have been suicide, yet he had a gut-tightening feeling that it made very little difference. Somehow he knew, very clearly, that Link Fannin didn't intend to leave him here alive.

Still watching in the mirror, past the bartender's sweating face, he saw Fannin look at Jim Taylor. "Well, kid?" he demanded, indicating the staring cattle buyer. "How about it? Is he ready to get you the money?" Young Taylor wet his lips and, not answering, he looked at the carpetbag on the table. The outlaw, following his eyes, exclaimed, "You mean he had it with him all the time? Hell! No reason why we couldn't of helped ourselves!" He added gruffly, "Well, no reason to wait. Grab that thing and let's be going."

The note of command in the rustler's voice prodded young Taylor; he actually put out a hand and took the bag from the table, but he remained where he stood as he demanded, "Why didn't you tell me about my pa? Why didn't you say your boys tried to kill him last night?"

"Now, where did you get an idea like that?" Fannin retorted, afterward answering his own question: "Or maybe that accounts for the sheriff being here. . . . So the old bastard *did* make it back alive! Well, kid," he admitted with a shrug, "the whole thing just slipped my mind. I wouldn't of thought it mattered a hell of a lot to you, anyway, the way I've heard you talk about him."

Ben Croft found his voice. "That's still not quite the whole story, Jim. This crowd's just been using you. Bud heard them say they have no intention of giving you any split of that money. I'm telling you the truth! You walk out of here with Link Fannin, and you're a dead man. . . ."

The outlaw's furious curse warned him what was coming then, and every muscle tightened against the expected smash of a bullet. But in the mirror he saw a most surprising thing. With more resolution than he would ever imagine, Jim Taylor swung around and hurled the bag of money at the hand that held the gun, knocking it aside; when the weapon roared, its bullet drove harmlessly into the floor. Fannin cried out and staggered back a pace.

Ben Croft knew it was the only break he was going to get. A frantic lunge carried him through the doorway, to pounce upon his own six-shooter lying on the floor of the veranda. Those posted outside had been waiting for him; he flinched as that rifle let loose again, but he had moved too quickly and its bullet came nowhere near him. By then he had caught up his own weapon and was turning back with it.

In doing so the toe of one boot caught on the threshold and he stumbled and fell heavily, with a savage wrench at his hurt shoulder. He saw the muzzle fire of Link Fannin's gun, saw Jim Taylor flung backward by the smash of a bullet, a chair crashing under him. Then, prone in the doorway, lying halfway across the sill, Croft propped both elbows against the floor and with the six-shooter braced between his palms fired twice.

The recoil hurt his shoulder and the spurt of smoke blinded him briefly. Through this he saw Link Fannin drop his head against his chest and start to go down, turning slowly as he fell. At the same moment a second rifle bullet, reaching for Croft, struck the closed panel of the door just above the sheriff's head, missing by inches. He needed no other spur to bring him lunging up and across the threshold, out of immediate danger. Turning, he saw one of Fannin's men running into the street, rifle in his hands; a snap shot from the sheriff's gun changed his mind.

Croft looked at the bartender, who had not yet moved during all this. "You!" he grunted, and going around behind the counter saw the sawed-off shotgun lying on a shelf below the bar, all loaded and ready for use. With an exasperated grunt he snatched it out and shoved it into the hands of the man, saying gruffly, "Whether you like the idea or not, you'd better get ready to stop anybody from coming in that door . . . unless you want to see your place torn to pieces! I know it's tough, but sometimes we don't have any choice!"

Not waiting for argument, he hurried back to see how it was with the two who had been shot.

A glance showed him that Link Fannin was dead; he turned then to Ed Denton, who was on his knees beside Jim Taylor. The cattle buyer looked up at Croft and shook his head. The sheriff knelt, knowing as he did that it was hopeless. Young Taylor's shirtfront was soaked with blood and the breath came quick and shallow between his parted lips; his eyes, half opened, plainly saw nothing. Fannin's bullet had done its job well. He only had minutes to live.

Looking up at Croft, the cattle buyer said in a shaken voice, "That took nerve, what he did! Even if he did lose the gamble!"

Unable to speak, Ben Croft could only nod.

His head lifted then, as awareness of a sudden increase in gunfire in the street outside shocked through his stunned awareness. Even as he pulled himself to his feet and headed again for the door, it occurred to him that he knew what it meant. He'd forgotten the Diamond T trail crew, but it wasn't to be expected that Gifford and the rest would stay out of this fight for long, once the guns began. . . .

It was Homer Ingalls who first caught sight of Ben Croft and the girl approaching the sheriff's office. In his shirtsleeves, with hands shoved into trouser pockets against the chill of the autumn day as he stood talking to Edie Bishop's father, he said something now and they both turned; they watched in silence as the tired horses came to a stand and Croft swung down from his saddle, to confront the rancher.

"Here's your girl, Bishop," he said. "We took an easy pace coming back from Flynn's Creek—spent the night at the Hawkins ranch."

Warren Bishop said gruffly, "Thanks, Ben." He stepped around the hitching post then to look anxiously at his daughter, who had made no move to dismount. She showed the strain she had been under. She did not look at her father when he reached up anxiously to touch her hand.

Croft said, "She's had kind of a rough time emotionally, but she's all right."

"We been hearing rumors," Homer Ingalls commented, "about the big time you had over there yesterday. Jim Taylor and Tom Andress both killed, we hear. . . ."

The sheriff gave him a look. "Bad news travels, all right," he observed dryly. "And gets worse as it goes! Yes, young Taylor's dead; but Tom wasn't hurt to speak of: just knocked out and trussed and thrown into a woodshed to keep him out of Fannin's way. Right now he's taking Jim's body home to his folks, and the money for the herd.

"Maybe it was really my job to do that," he went on, half to himself. "But I did have the girl to look after, and I didn't argue too much when Tom offered to break the news to the Taylors. I never thought I'd feel sorry for Bud Taylor . . . but with all his wealth and all his cattle, how much can it really be worth to him now that his son's dead?"

Breaking in on his somber mood, Homer asked, "What about Link Fannin and his outfit?"

"The Diamond T boys helped round them up. Fannin and Cash Agard were both killed. I figured it would be hard getting a conviction on the others, so I turned them loose.

But they know what will happen if any of them dares to show his face in this country again!"

Warren Bishop wagged his head, his blue eyes troubled. "Terrible things go on!" he murmured. "Terrible! All that matters to me right now, though, is that my girl is safe. . . ."

Ben Croft had unlashed Edie's straw suitcase from his saddlestrings; Bishop accepted it with a nod and hung it to the saddlehorn of his own horse, which was waiting nearby. Edie still had not moved or spoken, merely sat looking down at the hands lying in her lap. Bishop swung into the saddle. Fiddling with the reins he hesitated, looking aslant at Ben Croft on the sidewalk; he cleared his throat.

"Uh, come around some time, Ben," he said. "We're always glad to see you; don't be such a stranger. Maybe you could drop out for dinner, one of these evenings. . . ."

The sheriff merely nodded. "Thanks," he said briefly. "We'll see."

Bishop seemed about to say something more, then he closed his mouth and clucked at his horse, turning it from the pole. Edie followed docile and compliant enough. She and Ben Croft had talked little during the long ride in from Flynn's Creek; now she shot a last, quick look beneath her fair brows, and glanced away again. The horses moved off down the windswept street.

Homer Ingalls looked at his chief, a brow lifted quizzically. "Well, now!" he grunted. "What's the matter with you? Don't you know an invitation when you hear one? Now that young Taylor's out of the picture, I guess you begin to look good to Warren Bishop. Anyway, he just gave you the inside track with his daughter—and don't tell me you ain't interested! Hell, I was under the impression—"

He floundered suddenly under the calm stare Ben Croft laid on him. The deputy hunched his shoulders and amended, with a rueful twist to his mouth, "I guess I'm under the impression it's none of my damn business!"

Croft said tiredly, "Would you mind running my horse

down to the livery for me? Tell Charlie to see he gets a good bait of grain and— Charlie knows what's needed."

Homer nodded. "Wait till I get my hat and coat. . . ."

Alone before the jail office, Croft looked at the dusty street and felt the draining of utter weariness through him. He had slept poorly last night in the bunkhouse at Hawkins' place; and before that, there'd been the hard ride to Flynn's Creek and all that followed. And there was the ache of his hurt shoulder, which took something out of him even though neither Homer nor Bishop seemed to have noticed that he carried himself stiffly and wore a bandage beneath his coat.

But tired as he was, there was a restlessness in him too. His hand on the door, he paused and then abruptly swung away. And he felt a growing eagerness as his pace quickened along the chill and windy street.

He turned a corner and there ahead of him was the big house—and Jane Lawry who, at that moment, had stepped out upon the porch. When she recognized him he saw her quick wave of greeting; the relief and gladness in her face, as she hurried to meet him at the gate, somehow eased the weariness in him and gave a welcome lift to his heart.